The Dream Years

THE
DREAM YEARS

VIRGINIA AKIN

CHILTON BOOKS

A DIVISION OF CHILTON COMPANY

Publishers

Philadelphia and New York

To
GARTH
ALAN
HUCK
KEVIN
KATY
REBECCA
IAN
VICKI

Contents

1

Lost Christmas

"IT'S snowin'," Arla said. "Look, it's snowin'!"

Will looked up, the silver rhythm of milk against the bucket momentarily broken.

It had indeed begun to snow—soft thick flakes in the chill twilight—just since they had gained the shelter of the barn.

"Yep," Will said, and rested his head against the cow's warm flank again.

The child's hoarse voice irritated him. He wished she was in the house with Hattie. It had been too many years since a little girl had followed him around at chore time.

But she'd met him at the door in scarf and cap, buttoning her old coat, and asked to come—the first time she'd offered to leave the house since Martha had brought her. And Hattie had given him a look—and here she was.

"Snow for Christmas!" For the first time since she had come, there was excitement in Arla's voice.

Will's heart gave a half beat, and a coldness almost like fear touched him.

"What's that about Christmas?" he asked.

"Snow for Christmas," Arla said. "Christmas tomorrow."

"You sure tomorrow's Christmas?"

"Oh, yes. I been marking it off on the calendar Miss Sims give me from the feed store," Arla told him. The eager homely face caught all of the last light of the day, the only white thing that Will could see in the deep twilight of the barn.

7

It was that time of year. But why hadn't she said something before? Another child would have been talking Christmas day and night.

He and Hattie hadn't kept Christmas for twenty years. The best they could ask was that the day pass like any other. It was something they never spoke of, to each other or anyone else.

"What you want for Christmas?" Will asked.

He didn't want to know, but he had to give some response to those believing child eyes beneath the unchild-like brows.

"A big doll," Arla said. "Not a baby doll—a little-girl doll with real hair and sleepy eyes. I can make dresses for her."

For a minute Will was intent on stripping, pretending to be too busy to talk. He had forgotten, until now, the exaltation in a little girl's face when she spoke of the doll she wanted for Christmas. For it was so much more than a doll. It was another being, alike and beloved. The remembering hurt like a pain in his chest.

"And you think you'll get a big doll, do you?" Will asked.

She considered, stamping her feet a little because of the cold. "Yes, I think so," she said gravely at last.

"And why do you think so?" He wanted it to sound kind, but some way his tone struck him as doubting and cruel.

"Because I never did before," she said slowly, "and next year I'll be too old for a doll. So I think I will *this* Christmas."

Will got up and hung the stool on its peg, and picked up the bucket of milk. Old Mott took a sleepy mouthful of hay. Turning the button on the door, Will thought, *Plague Martha Sims. Dumping the kid here like this and never a word about Christmas. . . .* Of course she was busy; the Welfare Department was real busy this time of

8

year, he guessed. . . . Still, she was the one who should have seen to it.

Neither he nor Hattie had wanted to take the girl, but Martha had put it so they couldn't refuse. She had paced about the kitchen with her toed-out, flat-heeled walk, hands in the pockets of her baggy tweed suit, tears actually damping the nervous, sad horse-face.

"If you could take her, Aunt Hattie, just for a while," Martha had said, "till we can find some place permanent to put her. I can't leave her where she was another day. If you knew— Oh, sometimes I hate this job!" she'd cried.

Hattie had said dryly, "Well, I s'pose I could give her a good scrubbing, and feed her up some, but I can't keep her long, Martha. You'll have to find her a permanent place right away."

Martha had gone striding out to the car, then opened the door with the faded WELFARE DEPARTMENT on it, got the girl and her baggage—a paper sack and a shoe box—and dumped them in the middle of the kitchen. They hadn't seen Martha since.

It was dark crossing the barnyard. Will found his free hand holding a scratchy darned-mittened one by the time they got to the steps. On the porch, in the light from the kitchen window, he saw Arla's face looking gravely up at him from under the delicate feathering of snow on her cap.

"Before you take your coat off, Arlie," he said, "s'pose you bring in a load of wood for the wood box in the front room. Take it in the front door."

In the kitchen, he closed the door to the front room quietly. Hattie looked up inquiringly from the stove where she was mashing the potatoes, her face flushed and pretty from the heat. He came over to her.

"Hattie," he said in a low voice, "Arlie says tomorrow's Christmas. She's been marking the days off on her calendar, and she's expecting a present."

"Oh, my stars!" Hattie said. Pain flickered in her eyes.

They looked at each other. "She's never said a word. Not a word."

She began to whip the potatoes angrily. Like him, she turned her anger toward Martha Sims.

"Martha should have done something," she said. "You'd think she would have, Christmas being so near."

They heard wood tumbling into the box, in the other room, and a door closing. Arla was getting another load.

"If you could maybe make up some cookies or something," Will said, "I could cut a tree. I know where there's a little balsam fir just the other side of the pasture."

Hattie hesitated, frowning. She lifted the plates from the warming oven, then set them back again.

"Maybe I could do that," she said. "There's those nightgowns and stockings and underwear I got from the mail order today. I was going to surprise her with 'em after supper tonight, but I could put 'em under the tree for tomorrow."

Heavy knit underwear, long tan cotton stockings, striped flannel nightgowns—he knew just how they would look, the new-flannel smell of them when she opened the package.

"She wants a doll," he said. "A big-girl doll with real hair and go-to-sleep eyes. She thinks she'll get it this year, sure. It's kind of a last chance."

At the closed still look of Hattie's face, he wished he had not spoken. For immediately there was another presence in the house. They both felt it: the doll, lying there above their heads, her dimpled hands stiffly outspread on the blue silk skirt, her eyes serenely closed, on the delicately tinted bisque face a sweet impersonal smile, forever turned to the blue-striped wallpaper lining the lid of the trunk.

Hattie's lips made a straight line, her jaw was set.

"Call Arlie to supper now," she said. She took the plates down from the warming oven and set them on the table.

Seeing the firm way her hands moved, the stern pose of

her head, he knew there would be no good in speaking of
it.

After supper, when the dishes were done, Arla came over
to him where he sat with his sock feet on the oven door.
She stood beside him for a few moments, watching him
tamp the tobacco into his pipe, before she got out what
she wanted to tell him.

"I know a Christmas song," she said. "Want to hear it?"

He looked at the odd intense face—the skin so white,
the ragged hair so black, the eyes so burningly blue. She
had none of the tints and contours of a child, but the child
looked out of her eyes.

"Sing it," Will said.

She clasped her hands:

> *"Away in a manger*
> *No crib for His bed,*
> *The little Lord Jesus*
> *Laid down His sweet head.*
>
> *"The stars in the sky*
> *Looked down where He lay,*
> *The little Lord Jesus*
> *Asleep in the hay."*

She hadn't got the tune quite right, and the hoarse little
voice broke on the high notes, but she sang it lovingly,
looking at him shyly as she sang.

Hattie came over, the flour sifter in her hand.

"That was real nice, Arlie," she said. "You better go to
bed now."

The child started to the door, and then looked back.
She was waiting for something—some talk of Christmas,
some assurance that it would be here tomorrow.

But Will couldn't say the words she wanted, and Hattie,
already busy measuring out flour for the cookies, seemed
not to see her.

11

"Good night," Arla said. She shut the door carefully behind her.

"I'll finish up the dress I was making for her," Hattie said. "I only got the handwork left to do."

It had a brown wool skirt, a tan wool top, from two old dresses of Hattie's, and it was like everything Hattie ever sewed, neat and stout, but homemadish. Good enough to wear to school, but not the kind of dress to give a little girl for Christmas. A blue silk dress with pink rosebuds embroidered in the yoke, like the dress on the doll in the trunk—that would be the kind.

Will got up and brought his boots and Mackinaw in from the back hall and began putting them on in front of the fire, dreading the dark and the snow outside.

"I don't like you going out after a tree tonight," Hattie said. "S'pose you was to get hurt, Will."

"It's not very far," Will said. "I know just where it is, noticed it last time I was up to clean out the spring."

It was farther than he'd let on to Hattie—farther even than he'd thought. The creek was swollen from the storm, the log across it ridged with snow in the beam of his flashlight. It had been a long time since he crossed the log in wet weather. He hesitated, balancing the ax, and swept his light around him. All he could see through the deepening snow was a scraggly pine or two.

The little balsam would be halfway up the slope, in a small clearing that had let it develop in perfect symmetry. He had noticed it last time he passed that way, not thinking consciously, as he used to, "That would make a good Christmas tree," but something deeper than thought marking it, all the same.

He'd have to cross over now if he was going. Another few minutes of hesitation and he'd be much too cold to make it.

He didn't quite know how he got across, or how he was

going to get back, but he found the tree. It was a little bigger than he remembered, and he was sorry about that, because it would be harder to carry home.

But this was the one he'd come after, and he began on it, chopping away the lower branches one by one as the light found them, to give him working space. The trunk at first seemed to resist the ax. For a moment he regretted sharply destroying this living thing, but the chips were flying now, fresh-cut wood on fresh-fallen snow.

Not until he was halfway across the log did he remember the ax leaning against a stump, with the snow closing over it. It was not like him to leave it there; he was a man who respected good tools. But he was not going back tonight.

His balance was poor with the tree under one arm— stepping from the log to land he guessed too short and stepped violently into space.

A sapling saved him and the tree; but as he pulled himself up the creek bank, his heart began to beat violently. He sat on a log and let the snow and the cold and the darkness wrap about him.

Arla would be asleep by now, warm under Hattie's quilts, and the doll would go on sleeping up there in the trunk —how many more years? He made up his mind he would speak to Hattie about it when he got home.

He stopped in the woodshed and picked out some boards to make a stand for the tree. The yellow light from the kitchen windows, slanting through the falling snow, made him feel warmer already.

It seemed to him he had been gone a very long time. But Hattie was only frosting the cookies, cut in the shape of stars and Christmas trees. She scarcely looked up when he came in.

"Soon as I finish with this," she said, "I'll bring down the ornaments."

He set the tree up in the front room by the window. Its

fragrance, more powerful than the fragrance of brown sugar and spices, filled the house.

Hattie came in with the boxes of ornaments. She set them out delicately, carefully, but they had lain away from the light too long; three of them crumbled at her touch. The tinsel was deeply tarnished, the star of Bethlehem had lost all its sparkle, but they put them on anyway, working silently together, he on one side of the tree, she on the other. Last of all, they clipped on the candles.

These candles had decked the last Christmas tree they trimmed together—but they had never been lighted.

"I'll light 'em in the morning," Hattie said, standing back to look at the tree. "It'll likely still be dark when she gets up."

In the kitchen, Will put some oak in the range and adjusted the damper, and Hattie brought the rocker up to the oven and sat down to her sewing.

Will spread his hands over the warmth. Now was probably the time to speak about the doll. But he couldn't bring himself to do it. He remembered that long ago he had wanted to give Velma's warm coat to one of the Sweeney girls, knowing she'd have wanted it that way. Hattie's response was something he would never be able to get out of his mind:

"I'd rather burn it than see another child wear it."

It was still up there in the trunk with the doll.

The next day Hattie had started making over one of her old coats for the Sweeney girl, and neither of them ever spoke of it again. . . .

Watching her plump pretty hands rhythmically whipping the needle into and out of the brown wool, he found that he could not disturb her now. But neither could he forget Arla's "next year I'll be too old for a doll."

"Hattie," he said, "do you think Ben Hubbert might have a doll there in his store somewhere?"

"If he did," Hattie said, "it'd be fifty years old. He's

still got the same old buggy whips hanging from the rafters he used to have when Papa took me in there as a little girl. And how would you get it here in time? You couldn't get through tonight."

"Maybe I could," he said, "if I was to leave right away, and take the truck."

He went over to the phone. Three longs and a short, that was Hubbert's store, written up on the wall by the phone.

"What's that? A doll?" Ben was one of those people who always yell into a phone. "I don't stock 'em any more. Ever'body gettin' theirs from the mail order now. You hang on a minute, though—I'll go look—might have one somewhere."

Hattie held up the dress, frowning at the hem.

"Seems like I got it a little too short," she said. "But I left plenty of hem in case I have to let it out."

A stick of wood settled itself in the stove, and the room seemed not quite so warm. It must be good and chilly, Will thought, out in that drafty store. Where in the world, in all that accumulation, would the old man look for a doll? And even if he found it, it would be foolish to go after it tonight. He was so tired that it would be very easy to fall asleep and end up off the road. . . . Maybe he could get up extra early.

"I'm sorry!" Ben cried. "Sorry, Will!"

After he hung up Hattie said slowly, "I could make her a rag baby, but she's too old for it, and when she's got her heart set on something else, it would be like a slap in the face."

She was embroidering a yellow daisy with a brown center on the front of the dress. Her brow began to smooth out, her mouth to soften with the pleasure of the work.

"You go to bed, Will," she said. "I'll be along pretty soon."

Yes, he'd have to go to bed; he was too achingly tired

to be any good to anybody tonight. Too tired to talk about the doll. But at the door, he turned.

"There's that doll up in the attic," he said. "It's just what Arlie wants."

Hattie's lips tightened. Slowly she shook her head. She did not even look up, and the daisy went on unfolding steadily in her hands.

There was nothing more to be said. Twenty years and she had not changed. . . .

It must have been three o'clock when Will woke up.

On her side of the bed, Hattie turned with a little sigh to sleep more deeply. Always in the night like this when he awoke and she slept on beside him, she seemed to him the young Hattie, grave and trusting, unmarked by age and grief. And he would lie there and remember that both of them were getting old, and many things that had been, until he drifted back to sleep. But this was different; the awakening was as if he had an appointment with himself.

The stairs had a metallic coldness; he was shivering by the time he got to the attic.

He knew where the trunk was, under the small window, and the keys hung on a nail behind the door. He did not need a light. In his own house he knew where everything was. He got the wrong key at first, and the second key stuck a little before it turned in the lock.

He raised the lid on the odor of moth balls, clean woolens, long-folded cotton and linen. He felt for the solid shape of the doll.

It was not there.

He thrust his hand among the layers of clothing, the paper-wrapped bundles, feeling to the very bottom of the trunk.

What had she done with it? Had Hattie guessed his purpose, before he knew it himself, and hidden the doll tonight? Or had she burned it long before?

16

When he awoke for the second time that morning, Hattie was already up. It seemed a good deal later than it was because the snow on the ground reflected all the thin light of the beginning day.

He did not get out of bed at once. There was a feeling of grief about this day. It came to him a little at a time as he dressed, shivering, sitting on the edge of the bed.

When he opened the door to the front room, warmth laden with the balsamy fragrance of the tree was a breath of the long-forgotten ecstasy of Christmas morning. Hattie had lighted the candles.

Anyway, he thought, he had given Arla that—the tree, fresh and magical, more radiant than any tree before.

The door of Arla's room opened, and she came out in nightgown and bare feet. In her excitement she had forgotten to put on the slippers Hattie was trying to teach her to wear.

It seemed to Will that she stood quite still for a very long time, her arms straight at her sides, her face turned to the glowing tree. And then she began to search, but only with her eyes, as if she dared to go no nearer.

Almost as soon as Arla, Will saw it, sitting against a package at the foot of the tree—dimpled hands outspread.

Arla knelt, her thin little profile white against the candle-starred dark, the wings of her shoulder blades sharp in the worn nightgown, her sleep-tousled hair sticking up in back.

Carefully she touched the doll's white pinafore, the crisp blue-and-white gingham dress, the slip edged with tatting, the lace-trimmed panties all made since last night, he knew.

She smoothed out its skirt. Then she picked the doll up and held it to her with the immemorial gesture of the mother.

Until now he had not noticed Hattie standing in the kitchen doorway. She looked fresh in her gray-and-white print dress, her hair, even this early in the morning, neatly brushed and pinned up. She came over to him, and did something she had not done for a very long time—something he remembered from the young Hattie.

She put her hand on his arm and, looking up, spoke to him seriously and confidingly:

"She could be a pretty child, Will, if she ever got to looking like she belonged to somebody."

He placed his hand over the plump hand that rested on his arm—as the young Will had used to do.

"I think she's beginning to look a little like it already, Mother," he said.

2

Magic

"OF COURSE, I'll never marry," Susie said. She sounded so tragic that I stopped kicking through the drifts of yellow leaves on Poplar Street and stared at her.

"Why ever not, Susie?"

She hugged her Latin book to her with a forlorn little motion. "Because I'm so homely. You know I'm homely, Muriel."

I wanted awfully to say, "No, you're not, Susie. You're really quite pretty." But I couldn't, even if I am her best friend, because it just isn't true. She is little and sort of scrawny, for one thing, and she is still wearing braces. She has the kind of hair my mother says is a shame it's not a boy's, for he could give it a crew cut and forget about it.

Finally I said, "You look interesting, Susie, and that lasts better. Besides, lots of homely women get married. Some of the homeliest women I know are married."

"Oh, sure," Susie agreed, "but look who they marry—leftovers!"

I was trying to think of an answer to that when Alicia Wentworth hurried past us.

"Hi, kids," she called, and smiled at us. Her hair is the same warm color as the falling leaves. She is one of those girls so perfect that even her little imperfections, like a slight lisp and a tendency to a sunburned nose, seem perfect, too.

When she had floated across the street and out of sight I said, "If only she were snooty or stuck-up or something, so we could hate her! Honestly, how do people get to be like Alicia Wentworth, anyhow?"

"Magic," answered Susie with a wistful smile. No one in the world could smile more wistfully than Susie. "You know, Muriel, when I watch Alicia going through her part at rehearsal for the class play . . . she's so beautiful . . . I want so much to be like her that it just seems I *am*. Then, when I look in the mirror, it's a shock. Sometimes I think that if I just knew the magic word—"

The one thing about Susie that would be pretty is her eyes, if she didn't have to wear those big horn-rimmed glasses. They are big, clear gray eyes with flecks of brown, and she has a very confiding way of looking at you.

We were standing deep in golden leaves at the corner of Poplar and Elm.

"Well," said Susie in a lighter tone, "I guess I'd better hurry home and study my part, all two lines of it: 'I'll see if she's in, sir.' 'There's a young gentleman to see you, Miss DeLacey.' What do you bet I switch 'em the night of the play, and nobody notices?"

"Oh, Susie!" I laughed. She turned and waved, and went on through the falling leaves. The sky was very blue, there was scarcely any wind, and yet the leaves kept falling. I watched Susie for a minute, kicking through the drifts like a little boy.

Susie's clothes never really fit. I think her mother just keeps in mind the size she wants Susie to be, and then buys her clothes to fit that. My mother has a theory that the whole McKay family is color blind. There were times when you really wondered. For instance, that day Susie was wearing a green-and-scarlet plaid skirt, a purplish sweater, and pumpkin-yellow socks. Not even Alicia Wentworth could get away with a combination like that.

At rehearsal the next day, remembering what Susie had said about Alicia Wentworth, I glanced over at Susie as she stood by the piano waiting for her cue. She was toeing in a little—typically Susie—and her thin neck was craned out. Even her glasses shone with wistfulness as she watched Wayne and Alicia doing the garden scene. I noticed something else, too.

Lots of girls think Wayne is the handsomest boy in school. I guess he is, if you like muscles and bright corn-yellow hair. But Susie was looking at him as if he were Apollo, Sir Galahad, and Gregory Peck all rolled into one.

I wanted to say, "Oh, Susie, honey, he doesn't even know you're alive, and he never will."

As I started over to her to break the spell, her cue came, and she went on. She played her part the way she'd always done it—no inflection in her voice, and without moving a muscle of her face.

"Next time try to put a little more life into it, Susie," Miss Harris said, without conviction. Miss Harris, who is pretty herself, doesn't have much patience with people like Susie. Junior plays always have a part in them for a Susie, and usually nobody pays any attention to it.

At the end of the scene Alicia frowned and pressed her hands against her eyes for a moment. Miss Harris went over to her at once. "Headache, Alicia?"

"A little." Alicia blinked her eyes and smiled.

"Nerves," said Miss Harris. "Believe me, I know." She smiled companionably at Alicia. It wasn't only that it was our first Junior play, it was Miss Harris's, too. She was just out of college, and she was beginning to get a little jittery herself. "Tell you what to do, dear. Go home, take an aspirin, and go to bed."

She put her hand up and very lightly touched Alicia's forehead. I knew how Susie felt, then. To be Alicia, and have Miss Harris put her cool, lovely hand on your brow, like an anxious mother! We all looked after Alicia enviously as she left. Ah, the star!

Next morning we were standing around waiting for Miss Harris to begin the dress rehearsal. We were all there but Alicia.

"Honestly, Susie," Miss Harris was saying. "I don't care if your mother did take it in some more—this maid's uniform still hangs on you like a Roman toga. Mabel, needle and thread, please."

It was then that Mr. Hoskins, our principal, came in. For a moment he appeared fascinated by the sight of Miss Harris stitching Susie into her costume. Then he remembered himself and said, "Miss Harris, may I speak with you?"

"Certainly, Mr. Hoskins." She got up and went over to the wings, looking up at him respectfully. Somebody giggled, because Miss Harris is so petite, and tall, thin Mr. Hoskins looked so funny leaning way over to tell her something confidential.

We didn't hear what he said, but we heard Miss Harris's anguished, "Oh, no!" and saw her put her hands over her face.

Bill Johnson rushed over and got her a chair. As he explained later, he thought she must have lost someone dear to her. We learned soon enough what it was!

As Alicia was getting ready to keep her appointment at Myrtle's Beauty Box that morning, her mother found her plastering on make-up, trying to cover the red spots that had broken out all over her face. Her mother put her to bed and called Dr. Sneed. The verdict was chickenpox. . . .

For the moment we were so stunned by the picture of Alicia with such an undignified, childish illness that we didn't wonder what would happen to the Junior play without its leading lady.

"We'll just have to postpone the play, Mr. Hoskins," Miss Harris wailed.

"Well, now, I don't like to do that." Mr. Hoskins began to polish his bifocals. "On such short notice, we couldn't notify many of the people who've bought tickets. And folks will be driving in from the country."

"But there's no one who can take Alicia's place! Really, Mr. Hoskins, there isn't." Miss Harris was twisting her handkerchief just as Alicia does in the last act.

"How about taking the part yourself, Miss Harris?" Mr. Hoskins' glasses beamed with inspiration.

Miss Harris has short, curly hair and, when she wants to, a baby-doll smile. To an older person like Mr. Hoskins she would probably look all right in the part. But she shook her head with great firmness.

"Absolutely not," she said. "Without me backstage to prop these characters up and push them on, there won't be any play."

Mr. Hoskins cleared his throat and addressed the cast. We were all standing around, looking stupid. "Uh—young people—have you any suggestions?"

"Muriel!"

I turned. Susie's spectacles were shining at me.

"Muriel," she whispered, "*I* know Alicia's part."

"Why, Susie, how can you?"

"I don't know, but I do."

"Muriel Willis and Susie McKay!" Miss Harris spoke sharply. "If you have something so important to discuss, won't you please share it with the rest of us? I'm waiting, girls."

"Susie says she knows Alicia's part, Miss Harris," I said.

22

There was a gasp from the cast, then silence.

"What!" Miss Harris exclaimed.

I repeated it.

"Oh, please, Muriel, don't." Susie was tugging at my sleeve, blushing in spots, as usual.

"Well," Miss Harris said briskly, "we'll soon find out about that! Come here, Susie, left center. Let me hear you repeat Alicia's last speech at the end of Act One. The 'Oh, Archibald, where are you?' scene. All right!"

Susie walked over to the spot Miss Harris had indicated and looked around uncertainly. She was wearing the saggy-baggy maid's uniform, which didn't help a bit. But when she finally opened her mouth and started speaking—it wasn't Susie at all! She went through the scene with Expression and Gestures, exactly the way Alicia did it.

"Hmm," Miss Harris said, and for the first time since she'd known Susie, she took a really good look at her. "All right, Susie, Act Two, the garden scene, beginning, 'Why, Papa, there isn't anyone else here . . .'"

Susie did that, and another, and another.

"All right!" Miss Harris stopped her in mid-sentence. "That's enough, Susie. The show will go on. Jean, tell Mrs. Slade to send me in a sophomore for the maid's part. Someone who can memorize two lines by six o'clock this evening; who will fit that uniform without any alteration."

"Well, now, that's fine," Mr. Hoskins said, smiling happily and rubbing his hands together. "Nothing to worry about here." He departed with a fatherly smile. If Susie had been Julia Mae Brinker, who weighs a hundred and eighty pounds, it would have been all the same to him—just anybody who could get the right words in the right places.

But not everyone felt that way about it.

"Miss Harris!" Wayne said. He was frowning down at her.

"Yes, Wayne?"

"You mean Susie's taking Alicia's part?"

"I certainly do," said Miss Harris.

"Then I quit!" Wayne turned around and started to clomp off the stage.

"Oh, no, you don't!" cried Miss Harris. It was really funny to see our little bitty teacher run after tall Wayne, grab him by the arm, and march him back. But nobody laughed. We'd worked so hard on that play. We were all wound up to concert pitch, and if it didn't come off that night there were going to be about sixteen separate nervous breakdowns.

"All right," Miss Harris said. "You and Susie are going to rehearse the whole garden scene, right now."

"I'll be the laughingstock of the school," Wayne croaked. "When I say, 'You're the prettiest girl I ever saw—you're lovely, you're gorgeous,' they'll die laughing."

"That's exactly what I had in mind when I picked this play—death by laughing for the whole audience! Look, Wayne, can't you get it into your head it's not *you* who's saying these words . . ."

Hope dawned on Wayne's perspiring face.

"It's the character in the play, Archibald."

We could see the hope die in Wayne.

"Now begin," said Miss Harris briskly. "You're looking for her: 'Miss DeLacey, Norma!' That's your cue, Susie."

But Susie didn't move, except to put her hands over her face. "Miss Harris, I can't." She was sobbing. "Really, I can't. Because Wayne—Wayne—" Her thin shoulders shook.

Miss Harris spoke through clenched teeth. "You're both going to do it," she said, "if I have to knock your heads together. Stop thinking exclusively about yourselves and think of somebody else for a change."

That did it. They went through the scene, Wayne mumbling, Susie's voice trembling, but getting all the lines right. There was one big, drawn-out sigh from the rest of us. We had a play after all.

Then Miss Harris started in on Susie. She looked her over the way you look over a dress you're going to rip apart and put back together again right.

"Muriel," she said, "call Susie's mother and ask her to find out if there's any possibility of her dentist removing those braces temporarily—no, I'd better call her myself. You phone Myrtle's Beauty Box and tell her to be ready to take Susie in about an hour—shampoo, wave, the works. Tell her what it's for."

When I returned after telephoning, Miss Harris was busy with the tape measure.

"Umm, we'll have to take them all in at the waist, of course. But we can fix that—"

"I'm just Miss Harris's size, almost," Susie told me. "I'm going to wear her clothes in the play."

She said it almost reverently. I felt a pang of envy—a very small one, of course, because Susie is my best friend. Miss Harris has the loveliest clothes.

I went with Susie to the beauty shop. Myrtle's eyes bugged when she saw her. "You the lead?" she asked, with emphasis on "lead."

Then she began to get the same remodeling expression that Miss Harris had had. She really did wonderful things to Susie's hair, including a rinse she said would bring out its gold highlights.

All the time Susie was having her hair and nails done, I was running through the play with her to see if she knew her part. She did!

But just once, when she came to the love scene, she stopped.

"It'll be awful, Muriel." She shuddered. "He won't kiss me. You know he won't, and when Don comes on and says, 'What do you mean, young man, kissing my daughter?' everybody'll laugh."

"Look," I said, "they're supposed to laugh then. It's a comedy, Susie."

"Not to me, it isn't," Susie said. Her hair was plastered to her head in tight pin curls, which makes even the prettiest girl look sort of scalped. She was as pathetic as a half-drowned kitten.

I felt awful the rest of the day, on my own account as well as Susie's. I was somebody's aunt in the play, complete with knitting needles and a ball of yarn. I'd been having nightmares about the yarn coming undone the night of the play and getting all wound around the rest of the cast.

By the time I got to the gym that evening I felt the way you do when you're going to have your tonsils out. You know it's going to be bad, but you can't wait to get it over with.

And then I saw Susie!

Miss Harris and another teacher were working on her, one combing out her hair, one doing something to her hem. She had on a darling apple-green suit Miss Harris had worn only once, and high heels. They'd taken away her glasses and put something on her eyelashes to make them look long and dark. Her hair, smooth on top and fluffed out at the shoulders, was positively golden. And when she smiled—no braces!

"Susie!" I exclaimed. "Where's your fairy godmother? I want her to wave a wand over me."

But Miss Harris was touching up Susie's lipstick, and she didn't even hear me.

You couldn't say she was really beautiful, of course, not even in Miss Harris's pink net in the garden scene. But all through the play she managed to do something I had read about a famous actress: she created an illusion of beauty.

And when Wayne said, "You're beautiful, you're gorgeous," and held her in his arms, I think he and everyone in the audience had the feeling that he was holding a fragile and lovely girl. Goodness knows, *Wayne* was no actor!

That was Susie McKay's night, the night the butterfly

came out of the cocoon. Almost everybody in town was there, and they loved her.

When it was all over and we were on our way home, with my little brother asleep in the back seat, and me so tired I just had to lean my head on Mother's best coat, make-up or no make-up, Mother said, "It's simply marvelous what a pretty dress and a becoming hair-do, and being the center of attention, will do for a girl."

Susie was different after that. We walked home from school together the next Monday afternoon, as usual, and I kept looking at her. I couldn't see where she actually looked too different. She had a new way of doing her hair, with soft bangs over her high forehead, that was an improvement. But the braces had been put back; she still wore the glasses; and she still had to hitch up her skirt.

But she *was* different. When Wayne came along and said, "Hi, Sue," shy, yet sort of admiring, as if she were someone really special, Susie didn't blush or stammer or anything. She just gave him a smile, and answered, "Hello, Wayne."

If I hadn't been there I'm sure he'd have carried her books; and if she'd been anyone but Susie, I'm sure she'd have been annoyed because I was there.

"I suppose you'll major in drama when you go to college, and end up a star," I said. "Gosh, Susie, you were really wonderful."

"I'm going to major in homemaking." Susie's voice was decided. "I really don't want to act, Muriel, not ever any more."

"But Susie," I protested, "you're good, really good. Everybody said so."

"The truth is," Susie said, "I can't act. That wasn't me in the play. That was Alicia."

After a moment she went on earnestly, "But I don't want to be Alicia any more. I just want to be *me*."

I found myself giving a little sigh of relief. There really had been something uncanny about that Susie-Alicia.

We walked along slowly, kicking an occasional dry leaf from our path. Then Susie told me the secret that was to make such a difference in her life.

"I used to think nobody could love me because I'm so homely," Susie said. "But, Muriel—" a golden leaf drifted down and rested like a promise on Susie's hair—"ever since the play, ever since Wayne kissed me, I *feel* beautiful."

3

The Walnut Trees

THE cottonwoods were already a shimmer of leaves; there were yellow-green buds on the sycamores; but the walnut trees outside Mrs. Hackett's narrow, lace-curtained windows looked dead, unstirred by spring.

> *Walnut trees are sad to me;*
> *I don't know why.*

"Jenny Lee," said Mrs. Hackett, kneeling bonily on the floor, her mouth full of pins, "if you're going to stand with one shoulder all scrooched up that way, I can't ever get this to hang right. Straighten up, please, if you possibly can."

Jenny Lee straightened up.

Mrs. Hackett rose creakily and backed toward the sewing machine. "I do believe one of your shoulders is just naturally higher than the other," she said frowning.

Jenny Lee shrank inside the pinned-up hand-me-down from Cousin Anne. Mrs. Hackett had always had a faculty

28

for making her feel grotesque, misshapen. Mrs. Hackett knelt again at the hem, pins darting in and out.

> *When I see them bare-branched in the spring*
> *I want to cry.*

"Your mother wanted me to get this done by Friday, but I don't know." Mrs. Hackett leaned back, squinting at the hem. "I promised Miss Mead some things for Friday, and I just can't seem to get this right."

Beneath the tired-voiced complaint Jenny Lee could discern Mrs. Hackett's thoughts: *There's some use to sewing for Miss Mead—so pretty, such a nice figure. But I don't know why I have to waste my time on you. A gunny sack would do just as well.*

"Turn around again," said Mrs. Hackett.

Jenny Lee faced the mirror. She looked at herself with dislike. In her mirror at home, that thin, young face, surrounded by the auburn-lighted hair, looked intensely alive, interesting. But she was only gauche and plain in this looking glass.

"Why don't you cut off some of that hair, Jenny Lee?" Mrs. Hackett asked. "A lot of the girls are wearing it short now. Looks real neat." She made Jenny Lee's hair seem as untidy and unpleasant as too long fingernails, or dirty ones.

"My boy friend likes me to wear it long," Jenny Lee said. She raised her arms and lifted the warm, thick weight of hair from her neck, not looking at Mrs. Hackett.

Mrs. Hackett made a "hmm" that was not quite contemptuous because not quite audible. "You're sixteen now, aren't you, Jenny Lee?"

"I will be in June."

Old enough to have a boy friend, said the jet-button eyes, the tight, pin-cushion mouth; *but I'll bet a dollar you don't.*

> *Walnut trees by an old house,*
> *Unpainted, leaning;*
> *The walnut trees still gray and dead*
> *When all the rest are greening.*

Jenny Lee looked back at Mrs. Hackett's narrow, unfriendly house. It was not leaning, exactly, but it could stand a coat of paint. Anyway, it wasn't Mrs. Hackett's house in her poem; it was a house in a dream landscape far away, unbearably melancholy, in some April Jenny Lee had never known.

> *Walnut trees are sad to me;*
> *I don't know why.*

The words stopped singing through her mind.

That was Applegarth crossing the street, going her way, in the green April afternoon, to the Hunters', where he boarded. She had had him last year for biology; next year she would take chemistry from him.

"Hello, Jenny Lee," he said. Mr. Applegarth was one of the happy people.

"Hello, Mr. Applegarth."

He fell into friendly step beside her, a short young man, very little taller than Jenny Lee, but stockily, sturdily built. "Well, Jenny Lee, you'll be a senior next year, won't you?" Mr. Applegarth made it sound interesting, meaningful. He had an up-at-one-corner smile and sun crinkles around his eyes, and everything about him—his brown eyes, his crew cut—was intensely healthy, clean, alive.

"Yes," Jenny Lee said, trying to adjust her pace to his.

"I suppose you'll be going to college after that?"

"No, I guess not," Jenny Lee said. "I guess I'll be getting married."

"Well!" said Mr. Applegarth, and for a moment he stopped, right there on the sidewalk, and stared at her hard.

His astonishment was no greater than hers. She could not imagine why she had said that, any more than she could imagine why she had told Mrs. Hackett she had a boy friend.

"Well!" said Mr. Applegarth again, and he looked at her as no one had ever looked at her before—as if she were no longer a child.

It was not an unusual statement from a girl in her third year of high school in this country town. It did not seem strange when Lorene, so sure and pretty, said it, or Dotty, who had been going steady since she was a freshman, or Mae, who had a mature figure and settled ways.

But it was something no one expected of Jenny Lee. She was the youngest girl in her class, studious, bookish. Everyone took it for granted that she would go to college and be a teacher, like her mother and her aunt.

"Aren't you pretty young to be planning on marriage, Jenny Lee?" asked Mr. Applegarth. And he went on looking at her as no one had ever looked at her before.

The words came glibly now. "I guess so," Jenny Lee said. "That's why our families don't want us to announce it until I'm through high school."

"Anyone I know?" Mr. Applegarth asked. His humorously quirked eyebrow invited confidence.

"No," Jenny Lee said. "He's in the Marines. He's overseas."

"Oh." Mr. Applegarth's tone and look took on an adults-together seriousness.

They were at the Hunters' gate now.

"Well, good luck, Jenny Lee," he said. "Be seeing you at school."

Last year's annual was on the window seat in Jenny Lee's room, on top of a hodgepodge of notebooks, old themes, old workbooks.

Jenny Lee knew just where the page was in the annual. It opened almost of itself. She stared so long at his picture that suddenly it became terrifying that a spot of printed paper could mean so much to her. He stood, smiling, at one side in the group picture, not so tall as most of the boys on the team.

Oh, I do love him. I do love him, Jenny Lee thought. *I'll love him always.*

She got the nail scissors from the top bureau drawer and clipped around the picture. Then she opened the little jewel case on the bureau and took out her locket. It felt cool and solid in her palm—that small, heart-shaped locket with the tooth dents dating from long-ago Sunday school. She had not worn it for years—the chain was barely long enough, now—but the picture fitted into it. She had a little trouble with the catch, and then it snapped shut. She fastened the chain around her neck.

"I'm glad Jenny Lee isn't silly about boys," Jenny Lee's mother had said not long ago.

Aunt Margaret, with her long face, her tight, school-marm hair, always more worldly-wise than Mother, had started to speak, then closed her lips.

The study lamp made a golden pool for Jenny Lee's notebook on the dark, polished dining-room table. Through the open doorway into the living room the two women's voices rose and fell—Aunt Margaret's quick and slightly harsh, Mother's soft and tired. There were intervals of silence while Aunt Margaret checked a problem in long division or Mother took pains with the lettering on a flash card for the slow-reading group.

Jenny Lee was not listening to them. She was writing a poem.

"Well, I guess Janet Mead finally made up her mind," said Aunt Margaret.

Now Jenny Lee was listening, for the name had caught at her sharply. Miss Mead had only to appear in the classroom and a kind of awe settled over everyone. She was so beautiful, strangely beautiful, with ash-blonde hair, short as a child's, revealing a head and neck of perfect loveliness. Her eyes were round and kitten-gray, so that when you looked into them, you were astonished to see them deep with grave thought.

"I suppose she'll go on teaching," Mother said, "at least for a while."

After a long-division pause, Aunt Margaret said, "I wonder if she'll ever regret her choice. If she married that Armstrong boy, she'd never have to worry about money."

"I'm sure she won't," Mother said quickly. "Bill Applegarth is a fine man."

A large blot trembled from Jenny Lee's pen, hiding the poem under a grotesque, spreading silhouette. It was not so much that she should have guessed these two rare people belonged together—Janet Mead and William Applegarth. It was more that somewhere, buried deep, she had known.

She left her notebook open, with the blot-ruined words in the golden circle of light, and went out of the room and found her way upstairs in the dark.

She closed her door quietly and lay down in the dark, careless of her shoes on the white spread.

Through her closed eyelids she could see the bare, dead-looking branches of the walnut trees, unbearably desolate. Tears rolled warmly over her cheeks.

When Jenny Lee left school after her last class, she meant to pass the science room without looking in; but the open door would not let her walk by.

And Mr. Applegarth was there, as he often was, head bent over a microscope. He looked up and saw her, and smiled, as if he were glad to see her, just as he had yesterday afternoon. "Jenny Lee," he said, and then, "I have something here I'd like you to look at."

She went into the room uncertainly and put her books down.

"Remember that culture solution we got from Dillon's pond last year?" His voice was eager and happy, as it always was when he spoke of science. "Remember the protozoa?"

"And the rotifers," said Jenny Lee.

"That's right. Well, here's a culture from the pond that's

been allowed to stand three weeks. See if you can tell me what these are—animal, vegetable, or mineral." He adjusted the micrometer screw with a touch incredibly delicate for such strong, square hands, and Jenny Lee leaned over to look.

Someone was tinkling apparatus in the chem lab next door; there were shouts from the tennis court across the lawn; yet she felt that she and Mr. Applegarth were completely alone—more alone than they would ever be again. I could tell him now, she thought. I could tell him the truth. But she knew she would never tell anyone.

At the bottom of the well of light, the yellowish green striated shells appeared, exquisite and strange.

"I think they're vegetable," said Jenny Lee. "Diatoms."

"Good girl." Mr. Applegarth looked at her with approval. "You know, Jenny Lee, you're a girl who would get a great deal out of college." He squinted at the diatoms for a moment, then removed the slide and slipped it into a small pan with other used slides. "Miss Mead showed me some of your writing," he said, "and I think —we both think—you have real ability. There was one poem called 'November' that I thought was very fine." His manner had become stiff.

Jenny Lee could see he was one of those people who respect poetry, even admire it, but are a little embarrassed by it. She thought of the poem he meant, written out of the aching sadness of an autumn dusk, when she had remembered dancing around a bonfire her father was tending.

> Wood smoke and a waning moon
> And a few small stars
> And an old ache remembered
> In old scars.
> Those autumn dusks were long ago
> And well forgot,
> But wood smoke draws around my heart
> Like a rough knot.

"I hope," said Mr. Applegarth, smiling a little now, "that you will go to college, Jenny Lee, before you marry."

The tears had started, and now she was biting her lip and turning her head aside. "I won't marry him now, ever," she said.

"Why, Jenny Lee!" Mr. Applegarth was at her side, alarmed.

"He's dead," said Jenny Lee. "He's dead. I heard last night." The grief that had been building up tore at her chest, choked and stifled her.

"Let me take you home, Jenny Lee."

Just as she lifted her tear-ruined face to him, the locket slipped from the broken chain and fell to the floor.

Mr. Applegarth picked it up. The traitorous catch had not held, the locket was open in his hand, and involuntarily he glanced at it. . . .

He closed it, and then he took Jenny Lee's hand and put the locket in it very gently. He held her hand clasped in both of his as he spoke to her. His face had reddened; he seemed somehow very young, with his face flushed beneath the stiff brush of his hair; but he looked at her steadily as he said, "Some day you will be a lovely woman, Jenny Lee, and someone will love you very much."

And looking up into Mr. Applegarth's clear leaf-brown eyes, Jenny Lee knew it was true. For the first time in her life, she knew it was true. Some day someone would love her as much as she loved Mr. Applegarth, and more—oh, unimaginably more. It was a promise.

The happiness in her was like a green branch, like a rich and full-leafed branch on the walnut tree, which in the spring leafs out the last of all.

4

Little Runaway

WE WERE eating dinner when my brother Craig interrupted something he was telling to stare at me with his sharp blue eyes.

"Mom, does she have to make so much noise when she eats?"

Now my sister Janice looked at me, too, with that expression that began as a smile and ended as a grimace.

"It isn't the noise, so much," she said; "it's the way she chews with her mouth open." Janice shuddered delicately and turned away.

My mother, serving herself last with the smallest chop, did not even look up.

"Try to be more ladylike, Molly," she said.

I, the youngest child, should have been used to such remarks as these from Craig and Jan and my mother—I heard them every day—but I never did get used to them.

Years ago, when Jan was in third grade, before I had even started school, I used to think that, when you were in the third, you were almost grown up, and now here I was, nearly ready for the fourth (if I was lucky—if God was good), and still they all treated me like a baby, a stupid baby.

The humiliated tears scalded my eyes, and I could not swallow past the lump in my throat. I reached jerkily for my glass of milk; it tipped over, and the milk ran across the table and dripped slowly onto the floor.

"Molly, go get the mop," my mother said tiredly.

"Pig!" exclaimed Janice.

The mop was too dry to do an effective job. 1 spent several minutes pushing the milk over the linoleum. It was the ugliest pattern in the world—white and orange flowers like unwholesome cauliflowers with blue leaves, set in dingy brown squares. There was no use, my mother had told my Aunt Jessie just the other day, getting a decent rug for the dining room until I was older.

"I hate you, you damn' old stinking linoleum," I muttered, but no one paid me any attention now. Craig had gone on with his narrative; my mother and father and Jan were listening to him.

After I put back the mop, I did not return to my place at the table. Instead I walked slowly through the dining room, past the heaped bowl of intoxicatingly perfumed strawberries on the sideboard, and out the door.

"Molly O'Mara," my father called, "strawberries!" It was a passion we shared. Other people like strawberries—my father and I were mad about them.

"I don't want any," I said.

"Oh, come now," my father said. I can see him just as he looked there at the table in his shirtsleeves, putting a coaxing smile on over the worry wrinkles—a rather small man, he was, with skinny arms and legs and the beginning of a little paunch. He wore his thinning black hair long over the bald spot on top—his one, minor, vanity.

"Oh, come now, Molly—strawberries!"

As I stood in the doorway, staring at them all through a prism of tears, I saw that my mother's chin was trembling ever so slightly, as it did when she was distressed. But she said nothing; not one of them spoke another word to me. And I turned stonily and went through the hall and up the stairs—slowly, for it seemed impossible that they could all just sit there and let me inflict this cruelty on myself. But they did, all of them—even my father.

In my room—mine and Jan's—I shut the door and stood with my back against it for a long time, staring at my sister's neatly made bed with the prissy pink ruffle, just so, and her doll, Claire d'Lune, sitting against the ruffled pillow, smiling prissily. There was something about Claire d'Lune that infuriated me, with her pink enameled cheeks, her stiff curls, untouched by anything but distant admiration. She was like a fake bon-bon.

I threw myself on my lumpy bed, felt around for the lump that was my ancient Teddy bear, and held him close to me. I had almost lost him not long ago.

"Mother," Jan had wailed, "does she have to have that mangy horrible thing in my room all the time? I'm ashamed to have my friends up here."

My mother had promised me a lovely doll like Claire d'Lune if I would give up the Teddy to some poor little child (a euphemism for burning him up). I had cried, screamed, threatened to run away. And so I still had him for a little while.

I was going to take him with me when I went to the Budleys', and I was going now, this evening.

I got up and from under the bed pulled out the old straw suitcase I had rescued from the trash heap when Mother did her spring cleaning. She didn't know, yet, that I kept it under my bed, with some of my father's old Oz books in it, and some smooth round bones, and a piece of faded velvet ribbon and a bunch of frowzy flowers ripped from a hat, and an ancient pincushion leaking sawdust, and a glass doorknob.

I debated about taking the Oz books (some of the pages were missing). Finally, I put them 'way back under the bed. There were plenty of books at the Budleys'.

Having no children of their own, the Budleys did not know that I was too old to be read aloud to any more, especially from a book of fairy tales, and when I stayed with them, Mr. Budley read to me every night.

The packing went quickly now. My Teddy bear; my beloved, outgrown rabbit slippers; my pink celluloid dresser

38

set, painted with tiny blue forget-me-nots, that Grandma Muller had given me for Christmas—all found a place in the suitcase.

I picked up the small hand mirror and looked in it, troubled, as I was sometimes troubled these days, by the Me I saw there—thin face, black hair cut in a straight bang, teeth that seemed too large.

Replacing the mirror, I went to the closet and hesitated before the row of neatly ironed dresses. They were hand-me-downs from Jan, mostly, with thick turned-up hems and awkward tucks here and there, and I hated the lot of them. Anyway, I wouldn't need them at the Budleys'.

For a moment I dreamed of the dresses Mrs. Budley had made for me, picturing them hanging waiting in my small closet in the little room at the top of the house.

There was the crisp watermelon-colored taffeta; you could actually smell and taste the freshly split watermelon when you looked at it.

"Look, Tom," Mrs. Budley had said, "doesn't she look like a little fairy?" And they had both admired me, thin little Mr. Budley and stout Mrs. Budley. Later, hanging the dress away in tissue paper, Mrs. Budley had said in her rich enchanting voice which is sometimes the special gift of the stout woman, "It's all right to wear hand-me-downs sometimes, but every little girl should have her own new little dresses, too."

I could see the other dresses hanging beside the taffeta —a brown-and-white plaid with a big collar; a red gingham, polka-dotted in black like a ladybug's wings; a violet chambray with "Molly" embroidered across the blouse in purple.

Something about the violet dress troubled. There had been a little girl named Irene in first grade who wore a dress like that with her name embroidered on it—a little girl with a sweet, frightened face and long light-brown hair that curled, pure gold, at the ends. And there had been a square, tow-headed little boy named Jimmy who was the

Farmer-in-the-Dell, and when he came to choose a wife, I had prayed, the prayer bursting my chest, *"Choose me."* But he had not even looked at me. He had chosen the child named Irene.

Quickly I closed the suitcase, snapped the locks shut, and began to pull it after me, out the door, down the back hall, down the stairs, across the back lawn.

The hole in our hedge where I usually went through was too small for the suitcase; I could hardly get it under. I was still tugging and pushing—twilight was coming now, and it was quite dark under the hedge—when my father called.

"Molly O'Mara, where are you going?" I looked up and saw him hurrying across the lawn.

I gave a violent push, got the suitcase under and began to wriggle under myself.

"You don't care!" I cried. "Nobody does!" I had scratched myself on the hedge, and I began to weep.

"Sure I do, Molly O." Gently he took my feet and pulled me back—like a little old rabbit, he said—and tried to hold me to him, but I made myself as stiff as a piece of the wrought-iron fence.

"Now, where were you going?" he questioned again, and I began to sob.

"I'm going to the Budleys'," I said, "and I'm never coming back. They've been wanting to 'dopt me for a long time; they love me; they don't hate me like everybody here. And when I spill something there, Mrs. Budley just says 'accidents will happen,' and she mops it up herself and doesn't act cross."

"I see," my father said after a long pause during which the night began to move into the yard and the only white thing I could see was my father's shirt.

"Molly O'Mara," my father said finally, "how would you like to go fishing?"

"Who else?" I asked suspiciously.

"Just you and me," my father said.

"When?"

"Tomorrow."

I still held myself stiff in the circle of his arm.

"Don't you have to go down to the shop tomorrow?"

"No," my father said slowly, "I don't *have* to go down there tomorrow. I think we both need to go fishing, you and I. We'll take off for God's country in the morning and see if we can't catch us a few trout."

"I'm still going to the Budleys'," I said. "Even if you take me fishing. Jan and Craig hate me; they just hate me, and I'm too much trouble to Mother."

"Okay," my father said. It was quite dark now, and without meaning to, I had relaxed against his shoulder. "If that's what you want, Molly O."

"I have my own room there," I said. It was a little room up under the roof, yellow, with yellow curtains. When you leaned out of the window and looked over at the meadow, filled with buttercups like beaten gold, you felt exactly like a butterfly leaning against the air.

"I see," my father said, and then, cheerfully, "Well, if we're going fishing tomorrow, we'd better go get packed up."

At first my mother said flatly, "No!" Drowned she said, and my death of cold, and eating heaven knows what, and all the more work for her when I was brought home sick.

But in the morning it was all settled; we were to go, and my mother had even found some of Craig's outgrown jeans for me to wear.

Just as we were leaving, Mother put her hands on my shoulders and looked into my face, the worry lines plain on her forehead. Then she kissed me, rather shyly, as she always kissed us children, or anyone, and told me to be a good girl and mind my daddy.

Parts of that trip come back to me vividly now, untarnished by time. . . . I remember the chill mountain dusk, and my father's and my eating the cold fried chicken my mother had sent, and thick wedges of apple pie, sitting together in the front seat.

I remember waking, after dark, to a country road in the round gold beam of the headlights, to glimpses of split rail fences twined with wild roses, a stone-tumbled stream overflowing with stars, the living flame of a wild creature's startled eyes, a weathered house bowered in leaves—enchanted landscapes that still haunt my dreams and that I shall never find again.

We stopped at an old house. I remember how brilliant the stars were in the chill night and how the yellow light shone softly through the windows and the dew-heavy branch of lilac that brushed our faces as we went through the gate.

The people in that house were friends of my father's, and very dear friends from the greeting they gave him, and yet I do not know their names, nor where the house was. In one of the big rooms a cedar tree grew up through the floor and through the roof, and there was a seat built at the base of the trunk. That I remember, and the tall men who smiled at us and were so glad to see my father.

And I find it curious to recall—although it did not seem strange to me then—that there was a woman there who was stout like Clara Budley, with Clara Budley's beautiful loving voice. She made much of me.

"So this is Ben's little Molly," she said, looking fondly into my face as I leaned sleepily against my father. "She wasn't much more'n a baby last time she was here. She's such a pretty little thing, Ben." She had Clara Budley's exact affectionate phrase for me.

We stayed the night in that house. I remember chill heavy sheets and great quilts pieced with scraps of wool and velvet, and sinking down in a feather bed, as in a cloud.

I remember dressing in the morning by lamplight and tiptoeing out of the still sleeping house into an apple-blossom dawn, filled with the rare excitement of early rising, dressed for adventure in my brother's old jeans and lumberjacket.

My father parked the car off the bumpy rutted road and made a little camp for us against a huge fallen pine tree and sat me down by the fire while he went to catch our breakfast in the stream.

I was starving by now; I recall wondering if a scarlet spotted toadstool growing near the log could possibly be good to eat and deciding against it.

There has never been a fisherman more expert than my father, nor a stream that leaped livelier with trout than that stream.

It was like magic to me—casting a tiny hook into a dark pool and pulling out rose-stippled trout to fry dipped in corn meal and sputtering bacon grease over a camp fire. My father had baked crusty drop biscuits in the old cast iron dutch oven he always carried on camping trips, and he gave me an enameled mug half filled with coffee from the fire-blackened coffee pot.

"Don't tell your mother or she'll skin us," he said, pouring canned milk into my cup. And when I had tossed the last fish bone into the fire, he said, "I thought this was the girl who didn't like fish."

"I do when *you* catch them, Daddy," I said.

We sat together after breakfast, watching the dying coals and the smoke drifting up into the sunlight that slanted through the trees. I leaned against my father, and for a second I was frightened by the feel of his heart beating in the thin cage of his ribs.

"When I was a little boy," my father said, pulling out his pipe and leisurely tamping the tobacco into it, "I never got to go fishing with my father."

"Why not, Daddy?" I asked, surprised, turning to look up at his face under the shabby brim of the old fishing hat.

"Well," my father said, "your Grandpa O'Mara was a

43

great worker, and he didn't believe in fishing—said it was just another way of being lazy. I guess he was right, too," he added with a little smile.

"Didn't you ever get to go fishing when you were a little boy?" I asked pityingly, taking his thin hand shaded with the heavy dark hairs.

"Oh, yes," my father said. "I used to sneak off and go fishing with Uncle Rob. He lived in an old mill about a mile upstream from our place. He looked like a pirate, handle-bar mustaches and all, and I'm not sure he *hadn't* been a pirate when he was young. The stories he could spin! He didn't believe in baths except in summer when you could go swimming, and he had an awful old pipe— lots worse than this one."

I laughed. "Daddy, did I ever see Uncle Rob?"

My father did not answer at once, and when he spoke, he seemed to be considering each word very carefully.

"I don't know, Molly," he said. "You see, Uncle Rob was a lot like the Budleys."

"Oh!" I gave a little sigh that was half disappointment and half relief and leaned back against him.

Ever since I could remember, the Budleys had been there, warm and loving, whenever I wanted or needed them, and now something strange happened. I could see them, as one sees a brightly colored picture in a book, but when I leaned near to touch them, and the dear house, and the meadow glowing with buttercups, they were flat; they yielded nothing, exactly like a picture.

I snuggled against my father, against the familiar shabby warmth of his old fishing mackinaw. I felt lonely with a loneliness I could not have named.

"You know," my father said, "lots of kids make up somebody like the Budleys or Uncle Rob—'specially if they're kind of lonesome and think maybe their folks don't love them very much."

I looked up at him. "I know you love me, Daddy," I said.

The sun-wrinkles rayed out from his eyes when he smiled down at me. "That I do, Molly O," he said.

He knocked his pipe out against a stone and tucked the pipe in his pocket.

"Sometimes folks love their kids a whole lot," he said, "only they just don't know how to show it, and sometimes the kids don't realize they loved them until they're all grown up."

"Oh," I said softly, on the verge of understanding something, and yet not understanding, either.

I looked around me at the shadowy forest.

"It's a long way home, isn't it, Daddy?" I asked.

"It's not so far, Molly," my father said gently. "Not so far as it might seem to a little girl."

I caught his hand and clung to it, and some of the lonesomeness eased out of me.

I slept on the way back. When we turned into our own driveway at dusk that evening, it seemed to me, waking from some confused dream, that we had been gone from home for a very long time. I had quite forgotten the big oak tree that sheltered our front porch.

And I had forgotten my mother—her thinness, the way her brown hair sprang into little curls at the temples no matter how she smoothed it back, the way her dark eyes glowed when she was happy and excited.

Busy with getting dinner as she was, she did a surprising thing. She sat down in the little rocker by the kitchen window and hugged me and said, "I missed you, Baby."

"I missed you, too, Mommy," I murmured, my face against her starchy gingham shoulder. Actually, I had scarcely thought of her all the time I was away, but now it seemed to me that I *had* been missing her somehow— missing her dreadfully.

"I fixed over Jan's blue plaid for you while you were gone," my mother said. "You can put it on after you've had your bath."

I'd always liked the blue plaid, but it didn't fit very well. "Room to grow in" was our mother's creed when she sewed for us children.

I pulled the dress back, holding it in a bunch while I studied the effect in the mirror. *When I grow up, all my clothes are going to be brand new and fit skin tight,* I promised myself.

"Oh, for heaven's sakes!" Jan exclaimed as she came into the room. She went over to the dresser as if she couldn't bear to look at me and began to brush her springy gold-brown curls.

"I had my eye on this dress for a long time," I said, watching her profile.

"You look like a scarecrow in it." Jan admired her supercilious expression in the looking glass.

Once—day before yesterday—I'd have been crushed if Jan had told me I looked like a scarecrow. I'd have cried, probably, and then gone away to the Budleys', where everything was the way I wanted it.

But now I turned and answered her, not defiantly, but with a calm sureness I'd never felt before. "You just say that because you're jealous," I said. "Because Daddy took me fishing, and he didn't take you."

"Oh, for heaven's sakes." Jan's scorn was so exaggerated I felt I had struck home. I gave my graceless hair a couple of swipes with the brush and went downstairs feeling pleased with myself.

At the table, our father had scarcely got out the "amen" when Craig began.

"What'd you want to take *her* fishing for?" he accused my father. "She couldn't catch a fish if one landed in her lap."

"Daddy took me along for company," I answered smugly.

"Company, hah! Some company!"

"You're jealous," I said easily and went on eating my favorite piece of chicken with appetite.

46

That night, when my mother tucked me in bed, I grabbed her hand and kissed it.

"Molly, baby!" she exclaimed, startled, and yet—so pleased, so tenderly pleased. Quickly she stooped and kissed my cheek.

Usually, my bed was a boat (for, most of the time, the Budleys lived on an island) and I would close my eyes and float away to them. But tonight my bed was just my bed, comfortable and comforting as the sight of our house had been when we came home. I compared it with that exotic bed, with its heavy quilts and white-painted, iron-curlicued bedstead, where I had slept the night before, and it seemed to me that I had been on a voyage to some country infinitely far and had only by a miracle returned.

My father was opening my door softly, and I raised on my elbow to show him I was still awake.

"Daddy, I want to kiss you good night."

He came over to the bed. "I s'pose you'll be packing up and going off to stay with the Budleys any day now," he said. I couldn't see his face clearly in spite of the moonlight through the window, for he stood on the dark side of the room, but I could hear the smile in his voice.

"Oh, Daddy," I said, "you know I couldn't really go and stay with the Budleys." I sat up straight in bed, shaking back my hair.

The moonlight was very white that night, and the catalpa leaves cast huge, magically black shadows across Jan's bed. Claire d'Lune was leaning forward slightly from her pillow, and in the moonlight she seemed to be smiling with a mysterious knowing sweetness.

And I felt something about this room, about this house and the people in it, that I had never consciously felt before. I felt exactly the way I did about the Budleys. It was a sensation of warmth, of welcome, of belongingness.

I reached up for my father's kiss and whispered, my arms tight about his thin, bent shoulders, "And anyway, even if I could, I wouldn't want to."

5

That Time, That Joy

"SUSANNAH!" her mother called up the stairs. "Hurry!"

"I'm coming," Susannah said, but she went on standing, motionless, in front of the mirror.

It was the hat that was all wrong, she decided. Not that it didn't go with the dress; it did. The dress goods—blue voile splashed with white daisies—had been bought with the hat in mind. But it didn't go with the old top-heavy gray bus that lumbered down out of the mountains once a day. It didn't go with anywhere she went, or anything she did.

Susannah's eyes went past the bright, beflowered image in the mirror to the picture—a page cut from a magazine —tacked on the wall by her bed.

In a flower-starred meadow, a dark young man with a romantic profile sat beside a golden-haired girl dressed in poetic green. Near them on the grass lay a hat—just such a broad-brimmed, creamy straw, decked with daisies and velvet ribbon, as Susannah was wearing now.

The moment she had seen that picture she had known that the girl was herself, just as she had known that the hat was hers when she saw it on its knobby stand in the store window—the first time she had ever bought a hat by herself.

Susannah sighed and took off the hat. It was not that

meadows were lacking in her life. Every evening it was she who drove the cow up from pasture, a meadow very like the one in the picture. It was just that there was never anyone to *see* her there!

She had worn the hat once, to the Fourth of July picnic last year. Even now, at the thought of it, painful color throbbed up in her face.

Always before at the picnic she had come in first in the potato race; had swung in the breath-taking swing out over the creek; and finally she had waded, shrieking at the coldness of mountain water, in Riddle Creek. You couldn't do any of those things wearing the hat; nor could you just casually hang it on the branch of a tree. She cringed at the memory of the boy with villainous freckles who had clowned about with her hat, making a mockery of its loveliness.

Susannah picked up a comb and ran it through her hair, springy from last night's curlers. If you asked anyone in her family—her mother or father or Benjy—the color of her hair, they would say, smiling, "Well, it's kind of a dishwater blonde." Oh, if that just didn't go to show! It was gold—dark, heavy gold, and it was wasted, all wasted, like the hat.

If only there were someone to notice the color of her hair, to see how beautiful she looked in the hat, to tell her —not in words, perhaps, but with his eyes—"I love you." Someone she could love too.

"Susannah!" her mother called again, her voice rising with each syllable. "You're going to miss that bus!"

"All right, I'm coming." Without quite knowing why, she put the hat on again, arranging the elastic band under her curls. She grabbed the overnight bag from the bed and ran downstairs.

Her mother looked up from a careful placing of bread pans in the oven. "If that bus is on time, you've missed it."

"It's never on time."

"Here," her mother said. "I've fixed up a little lunch for you to take."

"Oh, Mama!" Susannah cried, revolted at the thought of food in relation to the Susannah of the hat. "I don't need it."

"You never can tell," her mother said. "They might not meet you on time."

"But I don't have anywhere to *put* it."

Mrs. Tipton opened the overnight bag. "You ought to have a little room in here," she said, "just staying one night." She slipped the package of lunch, wrapped in a double thickness of the Hodding *Weekly Courier*, in beside Susannah's new pink batiste nightgown.

"There!" her mother snapped the bag shut. "Now for heaven's sakes, hurry." She kissed Susannah briskly. "You look real nice." Her eyes lingered on the hat, but she made no comment.

Running, Susannah saw it had been a mistake to wear her good shoes on that dusty road. She should have carried them down to Yancey's and put them on there. Darn heels—hard to run in.

She stopped, panting, in sight of Yancey's sign: GENERAL MERCHANDISE AND RIDDLE CREEK POST OFFICE. She had only to cross the highway now and buy a ticket for Oak Bend. But as she stood there in the dust, getting her breath, the shabby gray bus lumbered into sight, slowed next to Yancey's, then rolled on.

"Stop, stop!" She was on the highway, screaming, waving her bag, but no one looked back at Riddle Creek. The bus, top-heavy with luggage, freight and bags of mail, rumbled across the bridge and was gone. Her hat had fallen at her feet.

Mr. Yancey was standing in the doorway of his store, and she felt that he was watching her with a pleased smile. People who sold bus tickets were always delighted if you missed the bus. She had noticed it before.

Mr. Yancey drew out his big nickel-plated watch. "Right

on the dot," he called. "You'd oughtta got up a little earlier, sis." He looked at her to see what she was going to do.

She had an almost uncontrollable impulse to slam her bag down and jump on it, and on her hat too; instead she picked up the hat, dusted it, put it on, and began to walk down the highway.

Behind her back, she could feel Mr. Yancey's stare of surprise.

It was silly to suppose she could walk the thirty miles to Oak Bend, but that was exactly what she felt like doing. All dressed up and no place to go! She was not going to trudge back home.

Purposefully, she walked past the Ellises', past the schoolhouse, past Van Dusen's garage and blacksmith shop, past the turnoff to Plassmeyer's ranch, and across the bridge where Riddle Creek came down in a white spray over the tumbled rocks.

Behind her she heard a truck thundering the timbers of the bridge. It was Mr. and Mrs. Mazzini with a load of hogs, on the way to Hodding, no doubt, this bright summer morning.

Mr. Mazzini slowed his truck, surprise and pleasure lighting his dark face to see Susannah, all dressed up in a big hat with daisies, walking on the highway.

Mrs. Mazzini, fat, comfortable and kind, leaned out the window. "Susie, you want a ride?"

They would be driving through Oak Bend, but she wasn't going to show up at Dorthiella's smelling of Mr. Mazzini's truck and all bitten over with hog fleas, which were the most ferocious fleas in the world. Not in that hat she wasn't!

"No. Thank you, anyway," she called, smiling falsely, and waved them on, as if it were perfectly natural for her to be strolling along the highway by herself, decked in her best.

She was still mad clear through about missing the bus,

but she was beginning to enjoy herself too. Buttercups and baby blue-eyes grew thick in the ragged grass on either side of the road, and a cool piney breeze touched her cheeks with a mysterious promise.

It was not until she approached the Worley place that she realized she couldn't just keep on walking down the road. Even before she saw the Worleys' steep-roofed frame house through the pine trees, she could hear the dogs.

"Dog isn't happy less'n he's got work to do," Susannah's father always said. There was enough work to keep the Worley dogs at a high pitch of joy twenty hours out of twenty-four, for they understood their life's mission was to frighten away all vehicles, animals, and pedestrians from the road in front of their ranch.

Susannah stopped at the first ecstatic yap. She knew how they worked. Two of them would be barking furiously in front of you, while the third crept around, silently, and attacked you from the rear. They were repulsive, yellowish, light-eyed beasts—"half collie and half hyena," Susannah and Benjy always said, rushing by in the safety of their father's car.

She could never get past them on foot. The Worleys ignored their barking as being no more than other livestock sounds about the place.

Susannah's palms were sweating, but her back rippled with chill. One of the dogs had slipped under the stock gate and was slinking along the ditch, ready to spring at her.

It was then that she heard the car. It came around the turn and moved toward her—a very old car, with a high top covered with ragged fabric, and the hood was off, revealing the pathetic, patched, rusting innards. It was laboring in noisy difficulty, and yet moving steadily onward, with a will more than mechanical.

The dog in the ditch saw it too, and leaped straight at it with a snarl.

52

"Help!" shrieked Susannah.

The car halted beside her, clinking and gasping. "Get in," the driver called over the noise of his vehicle.

She began to fumble with the door even as she saw that it was wired shut.

"You have to climb over," the boy directed angrily.

She leaped to the running board and clambered over the door half a second ahead of the snap of yellowish fangs. The car rattled and labored on, leaving the Worleys' dogs in a frustrated fury of malevolent yapping.

Susannah clutched her bag with one hand, her hat with the other. She could see a ribbon of road unwinding through a hole in the floor boards. The front seat was covered with an old blanket.

She stole a look at the boy who was driving. About her age, she guessed—maybe older. She saw a squarish face, grimed from living with that car, a brush of blond hair almost the color of her own, and a look of overwhelming purpose: to keep that car running. He knew it all by heart —every bolt, every drop of grease—and it was his will that was keeping it going, holding it together.

Never ride with strangers. I don't care how nice they may seem or what they tell you, Susannah—never get in a car with a stranger. Understand?

Yes, Mama.

The boy turned for a moment to face her worried stare, and she looked into gray, surprisingly dark-lashed eyes. In them she saw only goodness, steadfastness, purpose, and her mother's words floated away in the breeze.

If Mama could see him, she'd know he was a real nice boy, Susannah thought, and she began to relax, as much as you could relax in a car like that. "I sure do thank you for picking me up," she said.

"That's all right," the boy answered gravely. "I know what it's like to be on the road."

Did he think, *could* he think that she had been hitchhiking? In that dress, those shoes, that hat with the brim romantically splashed with daisies? Even if she could talk over the noisy laboring of the engine, how could she explain what she had really been doing out there on the road? She didn't know herself.

The boy was wearing a chambray work shirt, washed to thinness and no color, and very old, dirty jeans that she doubted had ever been washed at all. On his feet were a pair of narrow, high-heeled boots. They were now much worn, but they had been well-made boots.

In the back seat of the car was a roll of old blankets fastened with leather straps, a saddle, and a cardboard box with the handle of a frying pan and a fire-blackened coffee pot sticking out of it.

Susannah's eyes went back to the boy. "I'm just going to Oak Bend," she said. "You know where that is?"

"You holler when we come to it," he answered.

It was now that the happiness began to take possession of her—a happiness that was illogical, quite out of keeping with the car and all that had happened that morning, but nonetheless real and intense. She wanted to go on and on, in this incredible automobile, with this strange, purposeful and somehow utterly familiar boy beside her, all day. She didn't care if she never got to Dorthiella's.

She didn't even care, for herself, when one of the thin narrow tires blew out. The boy guided the wobbling car to the side of the road, stopped and got out to survey the damage. He sighed. "I'll just have to patch it up."

"Can I help?" Susannah was out of the car, eager, beside him.

"No, thanks. You got that pretty dress on." He blushed. "You just set and rest somewhere while I do it. Been having blowouts all the way down."

Susannah waited on a rock beside a stream in dogwood-dappled shade.

When finally the tire was patched and back on the car,

the boy lay full length on the rock beside Susannah, lathered his face and hands in the icy water with a sliver of soap, and splashed them clean.

With his face washed he was a good-looking boy. Even her mother would have had to admit that, Susannah thought, and Mama's standards were high, for she compared everyone with Susannah's father—who had been, when her mother married him, the handsomest man in Corazones County.

When the stream had cleared, the boy drank from his cupped hands.

Susannah was smitten painfully with a memory of herself and Benjy out fishing, losing their lunch of cold biscuits, bacon and jelly in Riddle Creek, and trying to stay their hunger with the melted snow water of the creek. It hadn't helped.

The boy was hungry.

"I got a lunch along," Susannah said. "Let's eat it now."

He blushed. "Thanks, but I don't want to run you short."

He'd be too proud to take it, Susannah thought, but she'd make him.

"I got plenty," she insisted. She ran to the car, came back with the paper-wrapped package and spread it out on the rock. "I just ate breakfast," she said, "and I'll be to my friend's by dinnertime. Mama made me bring it, just in case."

He ate the fried-ham sandwiches, the hard-boiled eggs, the cookies, trying to go slowly, trying to hide how hungry he was. Susannah ate one of the apples to keep him company.

There was such a strange ache in her because he had been so hungry. She felt that the hurt could be healed only by holding that rough head tight against her breast; she was amazed and a little frightened by that feeling.

When he had eaten, the boy leaned back against the

tree that sheltered the rock, hands clasped around his knees. His eyes searched out her face gently, carefully, as if trying to learn it by heart. "I guess I don't know your name," he said.

"Susannah. Susannah Tipton."

"That's pretty," the boy said.

"It's old-fashioned," Susannah said deprecatingly.

"It's pretty, though. I'm Rome Weitzel, short for Jerome. That's old-fashioned too, I guess."

"It's nice," Susannah said. "It's a real nice name." She had never known a boy named Jerome before, and she was glad. His name should be only his.

Susannah wanted to help push the car to get it started, but he wouldn't let her. "I done it plenty of times by myself," he said, and so she sat in the front seat, and when he had the car rolling he leaped over the door, grabbed the steering wheel, pulled the bent piece of wire that worked the choke, and got the engine going.

It seemed no time at all, now, before they saw the long, faded red building that was the Oak Bend Store and Post Office. "I guess I got to say good-by here," Susannah said.

He chose the top of a slope to stop the car on, and killed the engine. "You sure you got somebody to meet you?" he asked. He looked into her eyes with a worried frown.

"I'm sure," she said.

The Arbuthnots' green pickup was nowhere in sight. Probably they'd gone back to the ranch when they found she wasn't on the bus. "If they don't get here pretty quick," she said, "I can phone the ranch and they'll come and get me."

"You positive about that, Susannah? I don't like leaving you here alone."

"I'm positive. Dorthiella's my best friend. All I have to do is phone."

"Susannah, I want you to promise me something." He

was making her look at him, his expression stern and gentle at the same time.

"What's that?" Her voice trembled.

"You got to promise me you won't hitchhike no more, ever. You don't know what a risk you're taking. You're lucky it was me came along and picked you up." His voice became lower, and he blushed. "I guess you just don't know how pretty you are," he said. "Now promise."

"I promise, Jerome. I'll never ride with a stranger as long as I live."

He clasped her hand, and his hand, work-hardened, stained, and chapped across the knuckles, renewed that strange, maternal ache she had felt back there by the stream.

"Susannah, can I write to you?"

"Oh, yes," she said softly. "Yes, you can."

From the wooden ribs supporting the ragged top of the car, he took a dull stub of pencil and a much-folded envelope. "You write down your address for me, Susannah." He indicated a space on the envelope.

In her clearest, most careful hand she spelled out:

> *Miss Susannah D. Tipton*
> *Riddle Creek*
> *Corazones County*
> *California*

"Now can I have your address?" she asked.

He answered with a frown, buttoning his shirt pocket over the refolded envelope, "I'll write you that when I get to where I'm going."

She climbed over the door, snagging her only pair of nylon stockings, and Jerome handed her her bag. "Goodby, Susannah."

"Good-by, Rome."

He wanted to kiss her, she was sure, but he didn't quite dare, nor did she quite dare encourage him.

She wanted to say, "I think you're the bravest, noblest person I ever knew. Starting out on the road in that car and making it run, just *forcing* it to run, and saving me from those horrible dogs, even with all the worry you have on your mind, and being so kind and gentle all the time. I don't think any knight of old ever came up to you, Rome Weitzel."

She couldn't say it, not now. Maybe in a letter she could.

She had a little trouble getting a call through to the ranch, and when she finally did Mrs. Arbuthnot sounded kind of huffy. "Well, then, how did you get here, Susannah?" she kept asking.

And when Susannah answered casually, "With a friend," she wanted to know all about the friend. But after a while she said that Mr. Arbuthnot would be down and get her as soon as he could. The way she acted, you'd think Susannah had missed the bus on purpose!

But then Susannah forgot all about the Arbuthnots. She sat on the worn, wooden bench on the front porch of the store, the all-too-pretty hat resting in her lap, and pictured how she would go after the mail down the dusty road. The way she thought of it, it would always be high summer, flooded with sun. And she'd find a letter, a bulky envelope addressed in pencil in that painful, jerky writing boys use when they're trying to write with extra care. She'd tear open the envelope and unfold the sheets of rough-lined paper. She'd never had a letter from a boy, except from cousins, and that didn't count.

When the Arbuthnots got there, Mr. Arbuthnot apologized for taking so long, and Susannah was surprised, for she hadn't known it was long at all. He was a skinny, weathered man, nice and easy-going, and Susannah was glad Mrs. Arbuthnot wasn't along.

Dorthiella's little tow-headed sister Carrie Mae sat in the front seat with her father, and Susannah and Dorthiella sat in the back of the pickup on an old auto seat.

"What happened?" Dorthiella demanded. "How'd you get here?" Her red curls danced with curiosity, but she understood when Susannah whispered, "Tell you later." And even then, Susannah decided, hugging to herself the thought of Rome Weitzel, she wasn't going to tell her everything. There were *some* things she wasn't going to tell anybody.

The narrow dirt road to the Arbuthnots' ranch wound steadily upward, leaving oak trees behind. In some places you could almost reach out and pluck daisies and cat's-paws growing in the clefts of the rocks that towered above the road; looking down on the other side, you could see the tops of pine trees and the glint of mountain water.

"Ooh, this always scares me to death," Dorthiella cried, "I can't stand to look!" She hid her face in her thin, freckled arms, but Susannah gazed serenely.

Once she too would have cried out and shut her eyes, but this was not the same Susannah. She would never again be the same, now that somewhere Rome Weitzel was thinking of her, as she was thinking of him. She felt that she could step buoyantly over the trees, over the rocks and water, and that she would be borne up by joy. . . .

A drifting mountain breeze lifted the hat from Susannah's lap and, in spite of her quick fingers, sailed it gently, effortlessly, away and down.

Directly beneath them was one of those flower-starred mountain meadows that are the jewels of Corazones County; and here, missing the reaching branches, the hat drifted down and came to rest, exactly as if a warm hand had taken it away and placed it there in the flowered grass.

At first there was a sharp twinge of loss, and then Susannah realized that it was fitting that the hat should lie there forever, and she was glad.

It was a hat for finding your love in, and for that only. It was not suitable, had never been, just as a hat. Now that she had found Jerome, she felt it was right that no one else should ever see the hat again.

At the familiar rattling of the pickup over the cattle guard, Dorthiella lifted her head. " 'Zannah, your pretty hat! Where is it?"

With an airy wave, Susannah indicated the direction in which the hat had flown.

"Well, my goodness, why didn't you *say* something? Daddy!" Dorthiella rapped on the window.

"*Don't!*" Susannah cried. "Don't you *dare!*"

" 'Zannah, what's the matter? Don't you want it?"

"Not any more, I don't," Susannah said lightly. "It was just an old hat."

6

Who Was Cynthia?

ONE evening after supper when their mother was spooning out tonic to the boys, Alan, the Jonathan-cheeked middle boy, said, "Mother, if this tonic is supposed to be so wonderful good for people, why don't you ever take any of it?"

Their mother looked at the tonic, which was black and gooey, and tasted something like cod liver oil and something like old burnt overshoes.

"Oh," she said, "this tonic is for children only. If I took it I might turn into a little girl again, and *then* wouldn't we be in a pretty fix?" And Jenny Jimson screwed the lid tight on the bottle and put it back in the cupboard.

Jenny was the thin kind of mother, with ginger-colored

hair and a nose that turned up at the end. She wasn't pretty, but the boys thought she was. She wore full skirts in different-colored stripes, and whenever she had house-work to do she rushed around as if she were dancing so that she could hurry up and get to something more inter-esting.

And so, that evening when she had finished clattering and rattling and swishing the dishes about in the kitchen, she sat down, on the sofa, sighing happily, with Alan on one side and dandelion-haired Huck cuddled plumply on her lap, and she sent Garth, the slim, wide-awake first child, to choose a book for the bedtime story.

The book Garth chose was "The Big Book of Russian Fairy Tales," and the story they all particularly wanted was much too exciting for a just-before-bed story, but Jenny read it anyway.

When she would exclaim dramatically, "I'm Baba Yaga, the bony legged, the witch!" the two littlest boys would cling to her delightfully scared, and look up into her face, to be sure—perfectly sure—that that eerie voice was really their mother's.

And of course they could not possibly go to sleep, even after they had been tucked in, and told to go to sleep, and had had numerous drinks of water against the desert voy-ages of the night, and had had the lights turned out for positively the last time.

So it was that, what with one thing and another, the youth bed collapsed, springs and mattress on the floor, head and foot leaning in toward each other, and Huck all tangled in the bedding. When the commotion brought their mother to the door with a slipper in her hand, Huck cried out, "See, I'n Baba Yaga, Bony Leg, Vitch!" and the contrast of his words with the plump little legs wav-ing out of the tumbled bedclothes was so funny that Alan and Garth, peering over the edge of the top bunk, were sure that their mother would laugh. But instead she or-

61

dered them down, and spanked them, and even gave Huck a swat where it would make him yell the loudest, and told them that Baba Yaga absolutely was to cease flying about their room in her mortar and pestle, that night, and every other night.

And so, when they were all settled in bed again, there was a good deal of defiant whispering and fierce giggling, and Garth said quite loudly that if their mother turned into a little girl again he bet she wouldn't be so bossy.

The next morning Jenny made a face when she took her first swallow of coffee and said it was awful, but she drank it anyway. Jason said it tasted no different from usual, but then Jason never complained about things around the house the way some fathers do.

That night at supper Jenny set her cup down and said she was going to change the brand of coffee at once, and Jason said from behind his *Science Journal* that that was a good idea. Garth just smiled a mean little smile at Alan, who smiled back uncertainly. For of course Alan did not believe, really and truly believe—and neither did Garth. But yes, perhaps he did. Perhaps they both did.

However, when Garth opened his eyes the next morning, he had forgotten all about it. He lay in his bunk wondering why his mother didn't come in and pull the covers back and say, "Up with you now!"

The house was dreadfully quiet. He couldn't hear his mother flying around getting breakfast, opening windows, and airing beds all at the same time, the way she usually did. The silence made a cold feeling in Garth's stomach.

He vaulted down from his bunk, very lightly so as not to wake up his little brothers, and tiptoed into the living room.

It wasn't until he had looked all around the still room that he saw the little girl standing by the fireplace. But the minute he saw her he knew who she was.

Her wispy pigtails tied with limp pink ribbon were the

same gingery color as his mother's hair. Her eyes were round and brown like his mother's, her turned-up nose was sprinkled with nutmeg freckles, and she had a half smile tucked in one corner of her mouth.

She stared at Garth and her expression was not surprised or frightened or anything except interested. It was not even friendly. She wore a blue and white gingham dress with a tear in the skirt, there were briar scratches on her thin bare legs, and her bare dirty feet looked as tough and weathered as an Indian's.

The child said nothing, nor did she move. She just went on staring at Garth with her bright round brown eyes.

But Garth by this time had begun to feel very sorry for what he had done. He had a most awful lump of lonesomeness for his mother inside him. He wanted to say, "Oh, Mother, I'm sorry." But he was sure from the look on that gamin face that the girl didn't know anything about what had happened.

It didn't seem right to call her Jenny, but he had to call her something. So he decided to give her the name he had always meant to give a little sister. He had heard it in a story once and it was very pretty.

"Oh, Cynthia!" Garth cried, and out of lonesomeness for his mother, he rushed over and put his arms around her, and some tears trembled out of his dark-lashed, golden-brown eyes onto Cynthia's gingery hair.

Suddenly there he was sitting flat on the floor, looking up at her. Cynthia had pushed him down. She looked at him with her hidden smile showing a little more, but she said not a word.

Garth picked himself up and went slowly into the breakfast room, leaving the little girl by the fireplace.

There was his father's lunch pail on the table, so he knew his father had already gone off to work and forgotten it, as usual.

He peered into the kitchen with a wild hope that his

mother might be there, but she wasn't. Everything was so still that he knew she hadn't been there since the night before.

Garth got some cereal from the cupboard and some milk from the refrigerator, because he thought breakfast might help the lump in his stomach, but it didn't. It didn't even help to read on the cereal box about all the prizes you could get by sending in just 15 box-tops and 99 cents, or vice versa.

He was finishing his second bowl of cereal when he heard the lightest of little running footsteps. Cynthia stood in the doorway.

"I'm hungry," she said. She had a big voice for such a small slim child. It surprised Garth and even scared him a little.

"Help yourself," Garth said, not very distinctly because of the cereal in his mouth.

He waved his hand at the things on the table. But Cynthia made a face, and with a light swooping motion she whisked the sugar bowl off the table and set it up in the cupboard.

"Sugar isn't good for you," she said, primly.

She ignored the gritty trail of sugar she had spilled across half the kitchen and danced over to the refrigerator, opened the door, and began to rummage around inside.

Now Garth heard Huck and Alan pattering about and they came into the kitchen, their pajamas all droopy, Alan yawning, and Huck's hair looking more than ever like a tousled dandelion.

"Ugh, sugar!" Alan said, wiping first one foot and then the other on his pajama legs. "I hate walking around in sugar." And he gave Garth a dirty look.

"I didn't spill it," Garth said sulkily. "*She* did."

"Who?" Alan stopped in the middle of a yawn, frowned, and began to look around the kitchen.

"Her." Garth indicated the open refrigerator door. "Cynthia."

Cynthia was invisible because of the thick white porcelain door, but they could both hear her distinctly, moving things about, taking the tops off things, and spilling something.

"Garth!" Alan came close to his brother, his eyes suddenly very bright, his voice hushed, "Garth—did it—did it work?"

"Sure it worked. Can't you see her?"

And just at this moment Cynthia appeared, holding in one hand half a pound of yellow cheese, in the other a jar of pickles.

When Alan saw her—ginger pigtails, torn gingham, brown bare feet—there came over his face an expression exactly like that of a baby who is given a kitten to hold for the first time—an expression which is half apprehension, half incredulous delight.

Softly, tentatively, he said, "Hello, Cynthia."

Cynthia did not answer him, for her mouth was full of cheese and pickles which she ate standing up, with the pickle juice dripping down her fingers.

"This is what I always like for breakfast," she said after a while, and when she had finished crunching down all the pickles she wiped her fingers on her dress.

"Cynthia," Garth said, "you'd better give Huck his breakfast."

Cynthia looked at the empty pickle jar on the drainboard.

"There aren't any more pickles," she said. Then she saw the half-eaten piece of cheese by the pickle jar and handed it to Huck, saying, "Here, baby."

"I'n not baby!" yelled Huck. "I'n beeg boy," which was what he always yelled when anyone called him "baby." He stood in front of Cynthia with his feet wide apart, his head down, glowering up at her from under his dandelion shock, but Cynthia did not even appear to notice his unbabyish glare, and after a time he took the cheese and ate it.

Alan ate some Bun-Crunches, and then Garth, who

could tell time, looked at the red clock on the wall and announced that it was time for them to get ready for school.

"I can't go to school this way—I'm barefooted," Cynthia said, and she stood up on her toes like a toe dancer and admired her tough, brown little feet.

"I know where there's some shoes maybe you can wear," Garth said, thinking of a pair of brown oxfords, up-at-the-toes and down-at-the-heels, but still too good to throw away. "They're in the Grow-Into-Box in the sewing room closet. I'll show you."

"I'll find 'em," Cynthia said, and before Garth could move she had disappeared in the direction of the sewing room. She had a way of moving so lightly and swiftly that her slim bare feet seemed scarcely to touch the floor.

Garth and Alan went to their room and got into their blue jeans and their red plaid shirts and slicked their hair down with water. They even washed their hands, although not with soap.

Then the boys remembered about getting Huck ready for Nursery School. They went and fetched him from the kitchen where he was finishing off the cheese, and they got out his little red plaid shirt and his little blue jeans, and the rest of his things.

Suddenly Cynthia appeared in the doorway of their room. She was wearing their mother's highest heeled shoes —her best pair—and over her gingham dress, which was none too clean, she had put a dress of their mother's—a black velvet dress with a big lace collar which their dad had given their mother one time when he thought it was her birthday.

Their mother never wore the dress because she said it was too pretty, but Garth had an idea she wouldn't want Cynthia to wear it, either. Only, if Cynthia wasn't their mother, who was she?

It gave Garth a most unhappy feeling to see Cynthia
66

posing there, half smiling, in his mother's dress and shoes. She had tied one of their father's ties around her waist for a sash, bunching the dress up over it. It was a tie Jason never wore, except by accident, for he said it would put anybody's eyes out, but still he probably wouldn't want it used as a sash.

Around Cynthia's neck was a long rope of pearls, and even with a knot in them they fell clear to her waist. Their mother had said that they probably weren't real pearls, but they certainly looked real, and not at all suitable for a smudgy-faced child like Cynthia. The black velvet dress and the high heels didn't look suitable, either.

"Well," Cynthia said impatiently, "I'm ready for school. Let's go." And she seemed about to take flight, even in the bulky dress.

"Wait a minute, Cynthia," Garth said. "You better get Huck ready for Nursery School." And he showed her his clothes on the bed.

"It'll be better if he just takes them along to Nursery and lets them dress him," Cynthia said. "Here, baby." And she scooped up the shirt and the jeans and the little scuffed shoes and handed them to Huck.

"I'n not baby—I'n beeg boy!" yelled Huck, but he took the things.

On the way to school, watching Cynthia haughtily *clickety-clacking* along in front of them, pearls bobbing, dress swishing, Garth began to hope that Mrs. Bonner or Mrs. Joy would send Cynthia home and tell her to put on something else.

But first they had to take Huck to his Nursery School.

Old Mrs. Tait stared and stared out her kitchen window, and a man in a car jammed on his brakes and craned his head out to watch Huck plodding along in his sleepers with a button missing in back. Old Mrs. Tait and the man in the car seemed to be staring at Cynthia too.

When the children got Huck to the Nursery School, they opened the gate and shooed him in. The teacher opened the door and Huck stood by himself on the porch, clutching his clothes. They could hear his teacher exclaiming "Well, my goodness!" all the way to the corner.

At their school, Alan went to his first grade room right away. Garth looked uneasily at Cynthia, standing there in the bunched-up velvet dress and the high-heeled shoes, with pickle juice on her face.

"What grade are you in, Cynthia?" he asked, hoping that she would say "second," so he could put her in the second grade room and forget about her for a while.

"Oh, I'm in the third," Cynthia told him.

There was nothing to do then but lead her down the corridor—*clack-clack-clickety-clack* in the high-heeled shoes and the velvet dress—to Mrs. Joy's third grade.

Mrs. Joy had a long nose, and her hair was done up in a doughnut on top of her head, but she was really very nice. She was nervous, though. There were forty eight-year-olds in her room, and forty eight-year-olds day after day would make anybody nervous.

Garth crept into his seat, which was in the back row. There was a vacant seat right in front of him—someone was always absent with a sniffle or chickenpox or the like—and Cynthia sat down there.

It gave Garth an odd sensation to look at the back of that thin little neck with the wisps of gingery hair that had pulled out of the braids, and the slantwise part of the hair, as if she had plaited it herself. Garth put his head down on his arms and made everything black. He couldn't imagine that skinny, bedraggled Cynthia would ever grow up to be anything like his mother, and even if she did it would be too late, because he would be grown up then, too. He wished that Cynthia was in the second grade.

"Garth," said Mrs. Joy sharply, "don't you feel well?"

He faced the daylight again. "Yes, I feel O.K." he said.

"Then sit up and sing," said Mrs. Joy, and she pursed her mouth, waiting for them to begin.

When they sang "Good morning to you" Cynthia's voice was so loud that Garth had to put his hands over his ears. "Sh!" he whispered, "*Sh!*" But she went on singing after the others had finished. She couldn't carry a tune.

After everything got quiet again Mrs. Joy began writing spelling words on the board. *Click-clack-scritch-scratch* went her chalk, and all the thirty-nine tightly grasped pencils were supposed to go *shr-shr-shr*, copying, but Garth was watching Cynthia. He didn't want to, but he couldn't help it.

Cynthia held out a wispy pigtail in each grimy hand, and she was wiggling her ears, slowly. They were rather large, outstanding ears for a girl, and the way she wiggled them, up and down, was wonderful to watch.

"Garth," said Mrs. Joy, "how many words have you written so far?"

"Not very many—" Garth began, but there was something about Mrs. Joy's pursed mouth and penetrating eye that made him amend it—"None."

"Then get busy," commanded Mrs. Joy.

Cynthia turned around and looked at Garth with an earnest stare from her round brown eyes. She raised her eyebrows reprovingly, exactly as Garth's mother did when the boys had done something they should have known better than to do.

Garth began to write the words:

    train
    never
    shoes
    people

and each word was smudgier and more lopsided than the last. When he looked up for the next word, he could not help but see that Cynthia had taken the box of crayons out of the desk, and that she was coloring each fingernail a different color—orange, purple, green, red—slowly and carefully. Garth reached over and grabbed the crayon box indignantly, and crayons went spilling and breaking all around the desk.

"Pick them up, Garth," ordered Mrs. Joy coldly, "and then go sit in the corner. Crayons during spelling period —the very idea!"

But Cynthia had managed to save a piece of purple crayon and when Garth, close to tears, peered up at her from the corner, she smiled at him with purple teeth. They looked particularly repulsive with ginger hair.

Garth made a savage face at Cynthia, and Mrs. Joy intercepted it.

"Face the corner, Garth," cried Mrs. Joy in a shocked voice. None of her third graders had ever made a face like that at her before, not even the very naughty ones.

Head down in the corner, smearing tears with his fists, Garth heard a furtive nibbling like a mouse might make —a large impudent mouse. He turned his head timidly, stealing a look, and sure enough it was Cynthia, chewing on his mother's pearls, and Garth couldn't stand it, even if they weren't real.

He darted from his seat and grabbed for the pearls just as Mrs. Joy turned from the blackboard. The pearls went skipping and scattering and rolling all over the room, under desks, chairs, tables, and children.

"Well!" exclaimed Mrs. Joy. "Well!" She was breathing hard, and her topknot was slipping to one side. She walked down the aisle and put her hand on Garth's forehead. "Are you ill?" she demanded.

"Sort of." Garth swallowed hard, and rubbed a fist under his eyes.

"Well then—sit down in your seat and try to keep from creating any more disturbance." Mrs. Joy was so upset that she went back to the blackboard and began erasing all the words she had just finished writing, pushing down hard on the eraser.

Cynthia turned around and whispered loudly to Garth, her brown eyes very round and innocent, "I think I swallowed considerable of the beads. Listen—you can hear them joggling around in my stomach." Slowly she raised up and swayed from side to side—and, sure enough, you could hear them.

However, Cynthia swayed a little too enthusiastically, and the pearls fell out of her pocket.

"You," Garth choked, "you. . . ." Quite beside himself, he got down on the floor on his knees and began picking up the pearls and putting them in his pocket.

"Oh," cried Mrs. Joy. "Oh! This is really too much! *What* are you doing?"

"Picking up pearls," Garth mumbled, but for once Mrs. Joy did not correct his mumbling. Instead she darted over to her desk and began writing very rapidly on the back of someone's spelling paper.

When she had finished she folded up the paper several times and handed it to Garth.

"Here, Garth," she said, "you are to take this at once to Mrs. Bonner—at once, do you hear, and she will call your mother to come and take you home."

"My mother isn't there today," Garth said, and as he spoke a chill spread along his backbone and shoulders, and into the pit of his stomach.

"Your father, then," said Mrs. Joy.

Garth stumbled to his feet, and head hanging, face hot, note clutched in his hand, started for the door.

Cynthia followed, holding up the black velvet with one hand, her snub nose in the air. Her shoes went *clump-clump-clickety-click,* and she took her time getting to the door.

Just as she was going out the door a little girl with fuzzy white hair, who never did anything naughty herself but saw all the naughty things the other children did, called out:

"He was fibbing, Mrs. Joy. Mrs. Joy, when he said—"

But for once Mrs. Joy did not even listen. She went over and shut the door very very firmly after Garth.

To get to Mrs. Bonner's office from the third grade room, you had to go down a long corridor, and then turn, and then down another long corridor.

Cynthia began to walk ahead of Garth, who was shuffling and dragging his feet.

At first she walked very quickly, clicking and clumping the high-heeled shoes. Then she began to run. She kicked off first one shoe and then the other, and her slim dirty little Indian feet carried her around the corner out of sight.

Garth started running to catch up, and just beyond the turn, he found his mother's black velvet dress crumpled in a heap on the floor. He picked it up, and when he held it against him it made an ache in his chest.

A little farther on he saw his father's tie. He stooped to pick that up, and when he raised his head, he caught just a glimpse of a torn blue gingham dress and flying brown legs and feet skimming down the front steps, and a flash of ginger pigtails, and then Cynthia was gone.

Garth leaned against the wall by the drinking fountain, clutching the dress and the tie. It was no use trying to run after her. She had disappeared as mysteriously as she had appeared. Where in the world would he look for her?

It was very lonesome, dusky, and quiet in the corridor. From somewhere Garth heard the sleepy up-and-down voice of the kindergarten teacher reading to the kindergartners while they rested. He could not make out what she was reading, but the sound of her voice made him sad.

After a while, Garth opened up the folded paper Mrs. Joy had given him to give to Mrs. Bonner. He thought he had better read it first, just in case.

DEAR MRS. BONNER, said Mrs. Joy in large angry writing, WILL YOU PLEASE TELEPHONE MR. OR MRS. JIMSON TO COME FOR GARTH AT ONCE? HE HAS BEEN ACTING VERY STRANGELY AND DOES NOT SEEM TO FEEL AT ALL WELL.

HASTILY,
INELDA JOY

Garth slowly and carefully refolded the note and put it deep in the pocket of his jeans.

He could not see any use in giving it to Mrs. Bonner. And he could not bear the thought of his father taking him home, and finding Jenny not there, and then asking him, in his trusting, absent-minded way, where his mother was.

Garth decided that, judging from the pain somewhere in his middle, it was almost lunch time anyway, so slowly and thoughtfully he walked down the corridor, down the steps, across the playground, up the street, and home. There was no sign of Cynthia anywhere.

As he neared the house he began to hope, wildly, that everything would be all right, and his mother would be ladling out soup and telling him to wash his hands when he walked in the door.

"Mother," he called, and then, faintly, "Cynthia," but no one answered. No one was home.

He put the dress back in his mother's closet, and the tie back on his father's rack. Then he went and lay down on the bottom bunk until Alan came tip-toeing in at five minutes past twelve.

Alan's eyes were round and scared.

"Where's Cynthia?" he whispered.

Garth sat up and brushed off the place on the spread where his feet had been.

"I don't know," Garth said. "She just disappeared."

Alan's eyes became even rounder and more frightened.

"Maybe the boa constructor got her," he said in a low voice.

The boa constructor was a huge green spotted snake which very probably lived under their house. Garth used to tell Alan about it when they were in bed at night with the lights out. And sometimes they could hear it slithering and bumping and coiling itself against the floor of their room.

"Oh," said Alan, and he sat down suddenly on his toy chest and burst into a storm of crying. "Oh! Why did you let her get away? She could of growed up to be a mother to us. Now we don't got any mother. Oh! Oh! Oh!"

"Hm," sneered Garth, although his voice trembled. "A fine mother she'd make. She wouldn't even get Huck ready for Nursery this morning. And did you notice what she gave him for breakfast? A hunk of cheese! Hm!"

"It's all your fault!" bellowed Alan. "And I'm going to tell Daddy. I'm going to tell him what you did!"

"You don't need to tell him," quavered Garth. "I'll tell him myself. So he can help us get her back. Oh, Mommy, Mommy!" And he put his head down on the bunk and joined his sobbing to Alan's.

Presently the two boys stopped their crying, wiped their eyes on their sleeves, and went into the kitchen to look for something to eat.

"We'll tell him first thing when he gets home," Alan said. "Won't we, Garth?"

When they got out of school that afternoon, they decided there wouldn't be any use in going home until it was time for their father to come, so they went to the playground and lost all their marbles to a mean kid in the fourth grade.

After that they searched through alleys, looking for good things people had thrown out with the trash, and what with one thing and another it was almost dark before they decided they had better go home.

When they got to their own gate—very dirty and out-at-the-shirt-tails and out-at-the-knees—Alan caught tight hold of Garth's hand. The lights were on in their house, and a delicious sizzling odor like broiling steak drifted out.

"I'll bet Mom's home," Alan whispered. Garth pushed open the gate, and the honeysuckle on the fence smelled heavenly sweet as they brushed past.

The two little boys crept up on the porch. Through the window they saw their father sitting in his easy chair, reading the evening paper. Huck was playing on the floor, pushing some blocks around and saying "Chug-chug."

And there was someone in the kitchen whirring an egg beater.

When Garth and Alan walked in their father said, without looking up from his paper, "Hello, sons."

"Hello," they whispered back, and tiptoed into the kitchen.

"Mom, Mom!" they both cried, and Alan flung his arms around her on one side, and Garth on the other, and they both hugged her as hard as they could.

Their mother dropped the egg beater in the meringue.

"My goodness, boys, what's come over you!" she exclaimed. "Never mind," she added, kissing them lightly, "run along, and we'll talk about it after supper." And she gave them each a little push.

She was wearing a ruffly white blouse with a red, white, and blue striped skirt, and her hair was done up in curls on top of her head. She was the most beautiful mother in the world, but they couldn't help seeing that she had rather sticking-out ears, a thing they had never noticed before.

At the table that night Garth asked, looking at his mother's ears, "Mom, when you were a little girl in school, did you wriggle your ears and cause a commotion?"

Their mother raised her eyebrows and made her eyes very round and disapproving, exactly like Cynthia's.

"My goodness, no," their mother said. "I was always very well behaved in school." She took a prim little bite of pie.

Alan was staring at their mother with a puzzled frown, and finally he leaned over to Garth and whispered, quite loud, "What I want to know is—where's Cynthia?"

For answer Garth gave Alan a meaning nod in the direction of their parents, and a kick under the table.

Their mother's small bite of pie stopped half-way to her mouth.

"Who," she asked, looking first at Alan, and then closely at Garth, "who is Cynthia?"

When Alan was thinking very hard he frowned and closed his eyes; the thick dark lashes made a most fetching contrast to the round, Jonathan-red cheeks.

"I think," said Alan intently, opening his eyes, "I think that Cynthia is something—is something like—the boa constructor."

Garth gave Alan another kick under the table. Their mother was not supposed to know about the boa constructor, either.

Their mother looked from one to the other with the "this demands an explanation" expression they knew very well, but just then Huck, who had been getting sleepier and sleepier, and slipping down more and more in his high chair, slipped chin first into his meringue, so that it looked as if he had a little white beard. Garth and Alan both pointed and giggled and then whooped, and Huck laughed sleepily too, and their mother said, "Jason, speak to the children."

Their father put down his *Science Quarterly*. "Hello, children," he said amiably. Then he went back to his quarterly and his dessert.

At this all three of the children began to laugh even harder, loudly and helplessly, and their mother, who was trying to clean off Huck's chin, shook her head and said, "Sometimes I don't understand these children. I just don't understand them at all."

7

Red-Cushion Heart

AS SOON as that tall dark building came into sight, half the light went out of the morning. He felt slightly sick at his stomach and was conscious of a dragging weight in his feet. He stared at the place steadily, and there was nothing about it that did not depress him—the gray building, the cruel, wrought-iron fence, the bare, hard-packed ground, even the leafless oak trees with their black trunks.

At the gate his nose began to run and he felt for a handkerchief, knowing he didn't have one. He looked around, wiped his nose on his sweater sleeve, and went into the yard.

Three boys in caps and mittens were playing shrilly over by the swings. Their faces looked red and raw from the early-morning cold, and their hopping about made him think of stupid little birds who hadn't had sense enough to go south for the winter.

He went up the concrete steps, which exhaled cold and dampness against his knickered, wool-stockinged legs, and walked into the hall. It was empty, and the great high ceiling, the dirty buff paint and a faint odor from the boys' washroom all made him feel as lost and alien as on the first day he had entered it.

His mother had been so sure it would be a fine thing for him to go to town school; it was one of the reasons they'd left the ranch. He could not bring himself to tell her how much he hated it—hated everything about it but Miss Linley.

And even in Miss Linley there was no sureness. There

was not a day that he did not expect to find her gone, replaced by someone grim, middle-aged, dull-garbed like the other teachers, like Miss Grubbs herself.

That was because of what his father had said one day when they had passed Miss Linley on the street: "So that's Terry's teacher! Well, she won't last long."

Indignant color had flooded his mother's full face under the stiff, unfashionable hat.

"I'd like to know why not!" she had exclaimed. "Terry thinks she's a real good teacher and so do I."

His father had explained, "Oh, sure, but she's too good-looking. Some young chap'll carry her off any day now, and that'll be one less pretty schoolmarm. Never fails." And the sun wrinkles around his eyes had deepened in a knowing grin.

Now, at the foot of the stairs, Terry thought of why he had come early this morning, and a little glow of comfort and pleasure thawed the coldness in his chest.

He took the paper bag from under his sweater and felt about among the ten-for-a-nickel valentines for the big square envelope, lavishly thick, with Miss Linley's name on it. It was so large it would barely fit through the slot in the top of the valentine box.

At the thought of that box, a tremor of pure happiness went through him. Miss Linley had made it like a red brick cottage, with little heart-shaped windows. He could hardly wait to push his valentines through the slot in the roof.

But halfway up the stairs he paused, his hand on the iron-cold railing, and peered down into the empty hall.

There was another big square envelope, not so heavy as Miss Linley's, in his bag. He had printed "Miss Grubbs" across it in cunningly disguised letters. Now would be the time to leave it, if she wasn't in her office yet.

He went slowly back down the stairs and began to saunter through the hall. He could see through the glass door that the office was empty. He pulled the envelope half out of the bag. If he slipped it under the door she might not see it. But to walk boldly into her office—

"Terry, no loitering in the hall!"

He jumped, thrusting the valentine back into the bag. Miss Grubbs' voice always made him think of a fingernail raked down a blackboard.

"Either go on up to your room or go out to the playground."

"Yes, Miss Grubbs." He looked up at her reluctantly, thinking that she looked just like a potato—a lumpy potato with a washerwoman topknot of gray hair and sharp, disapproving eyes and a tight little mouth.

"Well, run on now."

"Okay, Miss Grubbs." He dropped his eyes to her shoes, special-posture shoes, highly polished, that looked as if she had put them on the wrong feet. He hated her.

Always sneaking up on people, he thought, going back up the stairs. You'd hear her voice at your shoulder suddenly, chillingly: "I will not have gambling in my school!" And all the marbles would be gathered up in her stubby hands, would disappear into her saggy black purse, and you never saw them any more. Everybody hated her.

Terry's hands were damp, clutching the bag of valentines. Suppose she'd caught him putting that envelope on her desk!

Miss Linley was not in the room when he went in—no one was—but he was reassured, knowing she had been there. There were fresh violets on the desk and a new arithmetic assignment on the board. She always had flowers on her desk, even when the children didn't bring them. Her boy friends gave them to her, the girls said knowingly, enviously, worshipfully.

Terry sat down in his seat and put the valentines on his desk, polished to satin with long use, carved with initials of boys he had never seen. He took out Miss Grubbs' valentine, and he felt a nervous desire to laugh, as he had when he was making it. He wished he had some other kid to show it to, somebody who wouldn't tell.

As soon as the first bell rang he would go down the hall, walk into her office, and leave it on her desk. That would be the only safe time, for it was Miss Grubbs who rang the bell, standing out on the front steps, marshaling them into line, grade by grade, and it always took quite a while. There were sure to be stragglers, little kids who got out of line, big kids who whispered. Just day before yesterday she had made him stand out there for ten minutes after all the other kids had gone in for talking to another boy.

He read over again with satisfaction the verse he had printed in big black crayon:

> *The devil flew north*
> *The devil flew south*
> *With old Miss Grubbs*
> *In his mouth.*
> *But when he found*
> *He had a fool*
> *He dropped her here*
> *To boss our school.*

But it was the picture that was the cream of the joke, a little masterpiece. Looking at it this morning, he could hardly believe that he was the one who had drawn that malevolent red-crayon devil with the snaky tail, the pointed nose and the evil horns. And Miss Grubbs—lumpy potato face, topknot, even the dangling feet in their ugly shoes.

"Good morning, Terry. You're early," Miss Linley said. He slid his hand guiltily over the picture. But she had not seen.

She went to the front of the room, her face gentle, half-smiling as usual, and began to pick faded leaves from the plants in the windows.

As always, for the first few moments he could not take his eyes from her—the wavy hair of that dark gold color that cannot be counterfeited, the clear profile. And this

80

morning she was wearing another new dress. It was the color you get when you draw your violet crayon steadily across your paper. He thought it the most beautiful color in the world.

Now was the time to put her valentine in the box. She would be sure to notice it, it was so large. Probably if he held it just right she would see her name on the envelope.

He pulled the valentine out for one last look, exulting in its richness. For a whole week he had gone back every day to make sure it was still on the rack at Jensens'. Finally, in an agony of shyness, he had handed over his quarter and asked the fat clerk to put the card away for him. It had been necessary to beg the other quarter from his mother.

She had taken it reluctantly from her purse.

"I know she's an awful nice teacher, Terry, but twenty-five cents is such a lot just for a valentine." She had weighed the coin painfully in her wash-ridged fingers a long moment before she had given it to him, and he had been ashamed because he dared not tell her the valentine cost twice as much as she thought.

But he had had to have it for Miss Linley; it was made for her. It seemed to him now that it didn't look quite as immaculately new as it had in the store, from being taken out and admired so often, and he wondered if he should get his eraser—

The bell rang insistently, angrily from the front steps.

Terry put the valentines hastily back in their envelopes, slipped Miss Grubbs' into his geography book, and hurried downstairs with the geography under his arm. The other valentines would have to wait.

The hall was empty. Terry turned the knob of the office door silently, darted in, shook the envelope from the book onto Miss Grubbs' desk, closed the door after him quietly, and walked out the side entrance. Taking his place at the end of the line, he was convulsed with a crazy need to laugh, and he put his hand up to his mouth.

"Terry, hands straight at your sides!" The voice like grating chalk—but for once it did not touch him.

Just wait, he thought exultantly. Just wait!

There was sweet luxury in the idleness, the murmuring, the spatters of giggles, now that all the valentines had been opened and they were marking time until the bell to go home.

Terry's eyes kept going back to Miss Linley at her desk, opening her valentines. There was such a warm goldenness about her against the drab room that looking at her made him feel almost as he had felt early June mornings up at the ranch when he opened his window and saw the west pasture shimmering with buttercups.

Miss Linley read the message of the card she had just opened, smiled and put it back in its envelope.

He had had to shove her valentine into the box hurriedly at first recess, so she had not seen it that morning. But she must have opened it by now.

The bell rang then, and half the children in the room rushed forward to her desk, pushing, stumbling against one another in their eagerness.

He knew what they wanted—to be thanked and praised, to have the valentines they had given her noticed—and so did he.

But he stayed in his seat, shoving his valentines into his bag, until all at once he could not bear the waiting and dropped the bag and went up to her desk too. He could see, over Susie Cramer's feathery towhead, the neat piles of valentines, even a heart-shaped box of candy. But where was his? It should be easy to spot; it was the biggest by far, and he had written her name very large across the envelope.

Miss Linley was talking with Helen Potter, who was fat and wore glasses and stuttered, and she was listening to Helen with the same loving, appreciative look she gave to all of them.

His valentine lay by itself, near the bowl of violets, almost at the edge of the desk. He reached out, squeezing past Susie, and touched the envelope, lifting it slightly by one corner.

And then he knew. There was no lavish weight of gold and satin and lace—only the flimsiness of two sheets of paper, maliciously scrawled. Without caring if anyone saw, he pulled at the paper inside until he could see a blur of red crayon. But he had known anyway.

When he got to his seat, he thought for a minute he was going to be sick. There was a burden of sickness in him that he would never, never lose. He found himself staring at one of his valentines. He crumpled it angrily and thrust it into his bag.

"What's the matter, Terry, don't you want to go home tonight?" Miss Linley was smiling at him, her head slightly to one side, as if she was fond of him.

He had not realized the other children were gone. He got up, and the empty room seemed so large he felt a little dizzy. He steadied himself at his seat before he walked up to her desk.

He spoke without having planned what he was going to say. "Miss Linley, I had a valentine for you, but I lost it. I lost it on the way to school."

"Oh, Terry, what a shame!" She put down her pen and looked at him lovingly and sympathetically. "What was it like?"

"It was great big," he said. "It was a fifty-cent one. It had lace around it, and gold writing, and in the middle there was a little door you opened and inside was a red satin heart, like a little cushion."

"Oh, Terry!" Her exclamation was half-admiration, half-regret.

Neither of them heard Miss Grubbs come in.

"Terry, here you are," she said. She was smiling at him. The lumpy nose, the small eyes, the tight mouth were all transformed by the smile, so that she did not seem to be

Miss Grubbs at all. She came over and stood so close to him he could see the "C.G." engraved on the fat little gold watch she wore on a black ribbon around her neck.

"I just wanted to thank you for my lovely valentine, Terry."

He could only stare at her, knowing his mouth was slightly open.

She held the valentine out to Miss Linley.

"Look, Miss Linley. Isn't it beautiful?"

Miss Linley took it and looked at it, looked at the "From Terry Higgins" written so carefully on the back, and her voice when she praised it was as warm and loving as it always was, though perhaps she had not spoken quite as quickly as she might have another time.

"Yes, it really is beautiful," she said.

Miss Grubbs turned again to Terry, and he did not think then of the words for describing her. But years later, when he recalled that time, he was to remember that her face had been girlish and soft and somehow shy, and that her voice was soft too as she spoke to him.

"I do believe, Terry, that it's the prettiest valentine I ever received." And then, confidingly, "When I get home I'm going to put it up on my bureau so I can look at it every day."

Terry stared down at his grimy fingernails. He had never thought before of Miss Grubbs as having a bureau where she might put something pretty, or even as existing apart from the school.

The silence after Miss Grubbs was gone lasted a long time.

"Terry," Miss Linley said at last, almost pleadingly, and he raised his head. She colored as she spoke to him, and there was a faint trembling in her voice.

"Valentine's Day," Miss Linley said, "is one of my very favorite days, because it's just for telling other people how much we like them or love them. Terry, I think—really, I am sure—that it was the spirit of love that made you get those valentines in the wrong envelopes. I don't think it was an accident at all. And, Terry, maybe some day you'll hear how it happened that Miss Grubbs doesn't have any-one of her own to love. And oh, Terry, you'll be so glad she got that valentine instead of the other one!"

She picked up the big envelope by the bowl of violets and held it out to him without saying anything more. Hot with the sick flush of shame, he took the envelope quickly, walked over to the wastebasket and tore the sheets of pa-per into pieces so fine no power on earth could put them back.

They walked downstairs together. A young man was waiting for Miss Linley in front of the school—a thin young man in a shabby car. Terry recognized him. He was the new doctor his mother had called the last time the baby had the croup so bad. The doctor's face was tired, as it had been the night he'd come out to the house, but when he saw Miss Linley something in his eyes lighted in a way that made him seem very boyish.

"I had a call out this way, and I thought maybe you'd like a lift home, Alison," he said.

"Why, Edwin, how nice!" To him too she gave her lov-ing, appreciative look, and then she turned and put her hand on Terry's shoulder.

"Edwin, this is Terry Higgins. He bought me a wonder-ful valentine and I haven't even thanked him yet."

She looked down into Terry's eyes. "Thank you, Terry." Then she bent, and he felt her lips like cool violets against his cheek and her fur collar brushing his chin.

"Is that the way you say thank you for all your valen-tines?" the doctor asked, and the smile that creased his face was as wistful as any boy's.

"Only the very, very special ones," she said softly. "Good night, Terry."

"Good night, Miss Linley." He began to run. When he

stopped finally and looked back, all he could see was a corner of the schoolhouse, a bare oak branch, and the tall iron fence, black against a reddening sky. He waited for the familiar sickening and darkening, but for the first time in all the weeks that he had been going to that school, they did not come. Instead, his whole being was filled with such sweetness and softness, he could not escape the feeling that somewhere inside him beat something like the little red-cushion heart that was hidden in the middle of Miss Linley's valentine.

8

The Deer

AS WAKE-ROBIN brushed out her hair in the clear light of that early summer morning, she felt fragments of her dream still clinging to her like petals from a wild plum tree. She could not remember it clearly, but the mood was strong on her still, a mood of extraordinary happiness, of bliss.

Her brown fingers moved with swift rhythm, braiding the long black strands of silken stuff, and she closed her eyes tightly for a moment, trying to look back into the dream, but all she could surely see was herself, slipping as she crossed the smooth stones of Aidenn Creek and reaching laughing for a hand; she could still feel the pressure of that hand, warm, strong, and masculine, on her own, smell the scent of a spice bush brushing her face, feel the damp spongy moss under her feet on the creek bank, and see, in a clearing lighted by a single plum tree blossoming into lace, a young doe poised with delicately uplifted head, her liquid eyes radiant with a wild woodland light. The sight of the deer had filled her with a pure, an exquisite happiness, and then she had been called from her dream, and she would never know whose hand had pressed her own, or why she had been so happy when she saw the deer.

"Wake-Robin!" her mother called, her voice rising strong and serene in the old house, and the girl answered absently, "I'm coming," and started down the narrow stairs.

A screen door slammed; she heard her mother exclaim, "Well, where have you been off to, so early?" and, after a pause, her young brother answering reluctantly, defiantly:

"Over to Dents'."

"Seth! You understood you weren't to go there again, as long as it's vacant."

"But somebody's there," he countered.

"There is? How do you know?"

"Well, I saw smoke over there when I was up in the barn-lot feeding the calves; so soon as I did my chores, I went over. I came out of the woods by the spring, and Peter was there, dipping up a bucket of water."

"Peter Dent!"

Wake-Robin's heart slowed, then began to beat suffocatingly fast. She clung to the stair rail, thinking with proud sorrow, *Always, it's always been like that, since I was a little girl.*

"Are you sure, Seth?" she heard her mother say.

"Sure I'm sure. He said, 'You're Seth Elliot, aren't you?' and I said, 'Yes. You're Peter,' and he said 'Yes,' and then I said I had to go."

"Was he alone, Seth?"

"I guess so. I didn't see anybody else."

Wake-Robin came into the kitchen yawning elaborately, hand over her mouth, and took her place at the long scrubbed table. Her mother flipped a final hotcake from the pan and set a plate before her steaming with the early-morning fragrance.

"I suppose," her mother said, half to herself, "he could be up here on his honeymoon."

"No!" Wake-Robin cried. "No!" She half rose; the sleeve of her robe caught the cream pitcher in front of her plate.

Without a word her mother handed her the wrung-out cloth for the spreading stain of cream, but she looked at her daughter sharply with the dark eyes that could always, if they chose, see more than you wanted them to see.

"We would have gotten an invitation," Wake-Robin said, mopping meticulously, not looking up. "I know we would. They were going to have a big wedding, and Peter always said we were just like his family. You know he did, Mama."

"People do change their plans, Wake." She spoke so gently that Wake-Robin felt her lips quivering, and inside her nose a sharp ache from the effort not to cry. When she could allow herself to speak she insisted with childish stubbornness,

"Well, I don't think they would. I don't think Peter would without letting us know."

Her father and big brother Kit came in with a noise of milk pails and boots solid against bare floors, wafting in the early morning smells of barnyard (in spite of meticulous brushing and scraping by the back steps), of crisp air, pine pitch, and the vigorous work of clean bodies.

They spoke to her teasingly in their deep voices, pretending goggling amazement at her early rising, the first breakfast she had shared with them since coming home from school, and she made herself smile and answer lightly, but there was something in their bright-faced unconscious pleasure in her presence that was a reproach to her.

"Better get dressed, Wake," her mother said. "It always takes you so long to do up your hair."

Her mother was always the same, Wake-Robin thought, at home or at school, knowing what you should do and expecting you to know it too, and to do it.

There must have been a note in her mother's voice that made Wake-Robin think of something that had happened when she was a little girl and her mother was teaching at the Aidenn Creek School—a spring day of flashing clouds and blue wind, when she, Wake-Robin, had looked up from her arithmetic to see Peter staring at her sister April with such a look—she did not want to remember it even now—a look of aching longing and love. There seemed always to be a light where April was, she so drew your eyes, awakened your happiness; and usually the thin dark little sister too delighted in April's golden beauty, shared in the warmth of her presence. Only she did not want Peter to look at April like that as she sat in a shaft of sunlight, smiling slightly over something she was writing, oblivious of them both. Peter belonged to Wake. He did not know it, but her heart had claimed its own when first she saw that sturdy boy with the red-gold hair, wide-spaced green eyes, and integrity in all his looks, in all he did, in the very movements of his square careful hands. And she had been glad with a dark hateful gladness that April was older than Peter, and that she was going away to school next year. Then, with all her strength, she had broken her pencil, a new yellow pencil, perfectly sharpened, and her mother, seeing, had exclaimed:

"Why, Wake-Robin, whatever made you do such a thing?" But she had not been able to tell, then or later.

"Better get a move on, Sis, if you're going with us," her father said, pushing back his chair.

"I'm not going," she answered quickly.

"Not going?" He came back, placed his thick calloused hand tenderly on her forehead, looked into her face, blue eyes warm with concern in their net of wrinkles. "Don't you feel well?"

"I feel fine. I'm just not going. There's something I have to do here."

She saw the signal her parents exchanged; her father shook his head slightly and his boots sounded sad going out of the room.

"Now what's all this?" her mother asked briskly.

"I want to see Peter, Mama." She met her mother's eyes, deep as her own, saw with wonder how many lines there were now in the Indian-dark face, how much white threaded the straight short hair she had always thought of as crow-wing black.

Her mother turned away without saying anything and began to scrape and stack the plates.

"You go get ready, Mama. I'll do that."

Her mother yielded, but at the door she said, "Wake, Tom Wilkins will be so disappointed when he finds out that you're not there."

"Yes, I know. I'm sorry." She poured scalding water from teakettle to dishpan with a steady hand.

Tom was like his name, with an earnest, round, ruddy face; whenever he looked at her there was a questioning hurt in his eyes. She felt sorry for that hurt, vaguely and distantly sorry, but no one on earth could keep her from seeing Peter, this last time she would see him alone.

Suppose Margery was with him! A chill like a cold wind went over her shoulders. She stood close to the stove, stretching her hands to the heat rising from the smooth black metal, watching how they trembled as if they did not belong to her.

She wished again that she had never seen the girl Peter had chosen. Almost she had cried out when she first saw her, last year in his mother's house:

But she looks like April! That's why you think you love her, Peter, because she looks like April. And she's not like her, nothing at all, inside. Can't you see that?

The physical resemblance to her sister was like a copy

not too skillfully done—the same blondeness, the deep dimples that go with a certain type of curly hair, the same straight carriage, although April's was instinctive and Margery's, you felt, required a special effort. Their eyes were not alike; April's were soft with a blue dreaming, Margery's more green than blue and narrowing when she smiled, and, to Wake-Robin at least, alien to warmth and lovingness. She was gay, was Margery, but April's magnetic happiness was not in her, only a kind of clever gaiety.

Oh, I've got to hurry, she said to herself. She left the dishes in the pan, turned down the damper, and ran from the kitchen without a backward look.

But halfway up the stairs she paused, gazing down into the living room. It was a big room, uncompromisingly clean, as was everything her mother touched, and so bare that strangers were often taken aback, embarrassed by its uncarpeted emptiness.

In this room, two years ago, April had been married to her Don, in a bower of lilacs against the south windows; here, borrowed chairs pushed to the wall, Wake-Robin had danced with Peter. They barely touched one another, their feet skimmed the floor, and she did not care how he had looked at April's shiningness that day; so everyone in the room had looked at the bride, and Wake-Robin went on dancing with Peter as if both of them were weightless, released from earth.

Later, with him on the porch, looking at the stars through the pine trees, his arm still lightly about her waist, he said,

"You know, Wakie, I was looking at you today, and I knew why your mother named you Wake-Robin."

"Oh, Peter, how lovely! No one ever said anything so lovely to me in all my life!"

She did not brush the tears from her eyes. It seemed to her in that moment that she cupped in her hand the half-open creamy flower, with mauve stains along its petals, for which she had been named; never had she felt herself possessed of so much beauty.

And then, just then, someone had interrupted them. Peter must drive his parents home. His father was going to die soon. Nobody mentioned it, but his face told you, it was so like a candle just before the flame gutters out, and he moved with such infinite care.

And he had died soon after. Peter had gone back to college, after missing half a year. And he had found Margery.

"No," Wake-Robin said. "No, no. Oh, my darling, no."

She must hurry, must run. She did not have time to pin up her hair. She let the heavy braids hang, but she did put on the blue dress she was to have worn to the picnic, and her pretty sandals, though they would be stained with road dust long before she got to the Dent place.

Once she stopped running, panting hurtingly, her hand pressed to the stitch in her side, and she thought: *Suppose Seth didn't see him after all? Suppose he only made it up?* Seth did not lie, really. It was only that sometimes he saw things that no one else could see. When he was four he had come running to tell them of a darling little snail-house he had seen in the woods back of the house; it had a tiny door, a wee window with curtains, a skein of smoke drifting from the tiny chimney. Even when they showed him the large thin book with the picture in it, he was not convinced. "But I *saw* it," he said, shaking his head, "I saw it out there in the woods." And only last year, he had come upon a cobra in the front yard. Choking with excitement, he had leaped into the house, describing the hood, the markings, the reared length of it, the evil, evil eyes . . . And when, more than half credulous, they all went out to look at the empty lawn, still he believed. "It was right here! Right here!"

Seth had a long brown Indian face, wide woodland eyes, like hers, a shock of Indian hair; he walked about silently in a world of his own. And she thought, despairing, *Suppose he did see Peter, but he wasn't really there?*

Wake-Robin walked on, her hand pressed into her side; once she stopped and unbuckled her sandal to lose a pebble.

And she began to think about the Christmas when Seth was two, when Peter's mother was sick and he had stayed with them. She could not remember anything anyone had said in all that time; only a quiet perfection, a loveliness clung to her memories of that Christmas Eve. Late in the afternoon, separated from the rest, she and Peter had stood on a hill above the house, a treasure of mistletoe in their baskets, with berries like drops of half translucent smoke. It began to snow; she held up a mittened hand to catch the flakes. And just then, below them in the wood, a window sprang into yellow life through the pine trees; hand in mittened hand they went down the slope to the cedar-shingled shelter of the house.

After supper, they all sat before the fire on their braided mats singing softly, half drowsily, to her mother's playing, Seth for once willing to be cuddled, leaning his warm weight sleepily against her with the bedtime sweetness of the freshly washed child. In the firelight, April's hair burned gold. And then their mother let her hands go quiet on the keys, lifted the lamp and blew it out, and beckoned them to the tall narrow south windows. Outside, in the slowly falling snow, a doe nibbled the hedge leaves. In the silence, she lifted her head, nostrils lightly quivering, a gleam of gold in the large liquid eyes. Peter held Seth up to look, and the little boy stared and stared with a wonder too deep for sounds or smiles. They were all quiet there together a long time, the clear Christmas music enclosing their silence, and Wake-Robin was filled with an overwhelming love that seemed it must break the bounds of her thin little body.

Oh, Peter, you belong with us. You did that night. You always will.

She heard the car before she saw it, an old blue sedan with the engine running noisily. Peter was closing the gate in the careful unhurried way he always did everything. It might have been any day, any time at all. He was alone.

"Peter!" she called. "Peter!" And, at his startled lift of head, "Seth told us you were here."

"Well, Wake," he said, putting out his hand, clasping hers. He was thinner than she remembered him—hair and eyes darker.

"Weren't you coming to see us, Peter?" She tried very hard for the right tone, light, without reproach.

"This is a flying trip, Wake." His clear eyes were steady on hers. "I'm supposed to be back on the job tomorrow morning. Spent all my time trying to get that old pump working. I'll have to send away for some parts."

"We could have helped," she said. "Dad and Kit—they'd have been glad to help."

A stubborn set to his mouth reminded her that Peter had never liked to ask for help, not even when he was a boy in school.

"Are you coming up on" (how hard it was to say) "your honeymoon?"

He hesitated so long with his answer that a wild hope began to pound in her chest.

He's going to say it's all off, it was all a mistake.

"I don't know," he said, "I thought we might."

If you fix the pump, her thought jeered. Because, of course, Margery could never carry water from the spring. I could, for you, every day till I died, but not Margery.

"And when is it to be?" (Ah, light and social tone, faintly bantering.) His answer, even, unemotional:

"End of August, I think. You'll be getting an invitation, all of you Elliots. I hope you'll come."

His face grew horribly distorted in a lens of tears.

"Oh, no, I won't come," she said, her voice thickening, "I couldn't bear to come. Peter, don't you know? Don't you know? And she—she—" But she was sobbing too hard to speak, and could not have spoken Margery's name in any case.

94

"Wake," he said, "little Wake." He put his arm around her, and unfolded his handkerchief for her groping hand. She moved away from him to use it, and sat down on a log by the creek, noting how thick the cress and waterweed grew out here in the sunlight, thinking she had not known there was cress here, before, and wishing passionately that she did not know it now.

Peter sat down beside her on the log, just not touching her, looking anxiously into her face, and she could not help the things she began to say; it was as if she had lost her mind, and did not care.

"Peter, do you love her?" she asked. "As much as I love you? Do you really love her? As much as you can love anyone? Isn't it because she looks like April? Oh, she isn't, Peter." She caught his hand imploringly. "Peter, if you marry her, what will I do?"

"My God," he said. "Oh, my God," and he looked down at their linked hands, hers thin and brown, his strong, with golden hairs. She saw that he was hurting inside too, and, horribly, she was glad.

"I can't talk about it, Wake," he said. "I'm sorry. I'm so sorry. Only, you see— You're so young, Wake-Robin."

He doesn't know what he's saying either, she thought.

She jumped up and her dress caught on a snag and tore, a long rent, and she was glad, because she would never want to wear that dress again.

"My love isn't young," she said. "I've loved you all my life. Don't you think children can love? And now I'm not a child, and my love is the same. Only more." She was shaking her head from side to side, her braids swinging against her, the way she cried when she was a little girl.

"Wake," he said, an arm on her shoulder now, "there are so many different kinds of love. As many as there are people." His voice was hoarse, almost as if he had been crying too, or was going to cry. "And if I said, Wake, that I loved you, and always will, then—I wouldn't want you to think it was the kind of love you wanted."

95

She was crying again. She couldn't see him.

"But it could be," she said. "It could be."

He pitied her groping then, and held her while she sobbed and, for the first time, she pitied him, pitied them both as if they were two children caught up in some sorrow they could not understand.

"I don't want to tell you this is part of growing up," he said. "My God, I think that's a terrible thing to say to anybody. We're all growing up till we die."

"Peter," she said, "do you remember that night, that Christmas Eve when we saw the doe?"

"Yes," he said. "Yes, I remember."

And after that, could hope still live? Yes, lived, sprang up again, until she saw the Queen Anne's lace, spreading its stiff white-over-green against the lower meadow fence. That would be like Margery's wedding dress, she thought: lavish, yet sharply outlined about the girl's beauty. She recalled the exact shade of Margery's hair; there was the slightest, faintest greenish cast on the deep waves that shone about her face and neck. And she remembered a certain look in Margery's blue-green eyes, the look of one who does not lightly give up anything she has ever held, who does not, indeed, give it up at all. She must have had that look from birth.

For the first time, Wake-Robin despaired. She twisted a floweret from the tall weed, staining her fingers with the poisonous scent. The ugly smell clung to her hands a long time, even after she had scrubbed them in the sink with harsh yellow soap.

It was while she was washing her hands that she thought that if Peter had been false to Margery, and taken her instead, he would not have been Peter any more, but there was no solace in that. She did not care in the least if he deceived Margery, or anyone, not even herself, if only for a little while he might have made her think he loved her.

She knew she could have lived on that little while all her life.

A thick brown book lay on the old spindle-legged table by her bed. Wake-Robin picked it up, reading her sister's name on the flyleaf as if she had never seen it before. It was a book her sister had loved; many a night the younger girl had opened drowsing eyes to see April bent over its thin pages in the lamplight.

"Go to sleep, Wakie," April would say, like a lullaby, and Wake-Robin, shutting her eyes, would think that none of the girls whose loveliness was sung in those poems could be half so beautiful as her sister.

A poem in this book had stuck in her mind once, like a little burry seed of understanding. Suddenly it became important that she should read it again; she could not remember the poet's name, but it was at the front of the book.

She began to read:

> *Whoso list to hunt, I know where is an hind,*
> *But as for me, helas, I may no more.*

She read on to the end

> *Noli me tangere, for Caesar's I am*
> *And wild for to hold, though I seem tame.*

She dropped the book, trembling as if with chill. When first she read those words, they had been only a poet's bearded face, fierce and defiant, and a year long, long ago, and now she knew that they were a voice crying in the next room, and all the voices of lovers bereft for ten thousand years broke her heart with their crying.

But that was not the sharpest pain. For now she faced the truth about Margery. In her anger and jealousy, she had tried to make Margery less, far less than she was. There was some mystery there, strange beauty she herself could never take hold of, loveliness that would haunt and elude her all her life. If only she had not seen her, never seen the blue-green eyes and the fresh perfect mouth and the white stalk of her neck, the way she looked at Peter, the way he looked—oh God, the way he looked at her.

> Yet may I by no means my wearied mind
> Draw from the deer . . .

She cried until she bit the corner of her pillow, and her sobs were harsh and labored in her ears. Finally, mouth open, face blubbered like a child's, she slept a little while.

She had awakened, thinking, *I have to get up, I have to wash my face*, when she heard the car drive up in front. For one wild pulse of hope she cried, "Peter!"

But even before she reached the window, she knew it was not he.

"Wake-Robin!" Tom Wilkins called up to her anxiously, searching the window with his kind, near-sighted eyes.

"Yes," she called, stifling a sigh, "I'll be down in a minute."

When she had washed her face, she was surprised how little trace the tears had left. Her eyes were only a little reddened and swollen. She smoothed her hair with her hands and went down to Tom.

"I just couldn't believe you wouldn't come, Wake," he said. "When your folks told me, I thought—well, I looked forward all winter, you know. I kept thinking you'd be at the Grange picnic."

He turned his ruddy face anxiously to her; poor Tom had a cast in one eye; while he held you earnestly with the straight one, the other wandered innocently afield.

"I could come now," she said. Her voice was still slightly hoarse.

"Do you have a cold?" he asked in quick anxiety. "Aren't you well?"

"I'm all right," she said. "I'm fine."

"You look different, Wake-Robin. Older, and—"

98

"Well, I *am* older," she said. Very gently, she disengaged her hand from his. "I'll be ready in a minute, soon as I change my dress."

9

Inspiration

Old Mr. Marlowe had three daughters; Heather was all silvery blonde, Hawthorne was dark as a forest pool, and Briar-Rose—

There was a knock, light and diffident, on Janet's door. She had not known, really, what she was going to write about Briar-Rose, but she waited a few reluctant moments before she called out absently, "Yes?"

The door opened, and it was her mother.

"I was going to ask," her mother said, "if maybe you could run over to the market for me, but of course, if you're Writing—" She looked respectfully at the paper on her daughter's desk.

Ever since Janet had won the Hattie Elkins Wisdom Memorial Award for the best essay by a Junior High School student, last spring, her mother had been capitalizing Writing in this way. And if her mother discovered that Janet had been overcome with inspiration while dusting or raking the yard, or even ironing her slips, she was usually excused from these tasks so that she might rush to her room and get it down on paper while the flame still burned. It had gotten so that the mere sight of an after-dinner table to be cleared away was enough to bring on a poem.

There was only one thing wrong with all this, and the

opportunities for writing and her mother's pride were making it more apparent every day: whatever Edgar Allan Poe, say, or Louisa May Alcott had had, Janet did not have, and never would.

Of course she could turn out poems, or maybe they were verses (Miss Sparrow said there was a difference), for Christmas, July Fourth, and Arbor Day, but so could hundreds of other kids in town. And, with a slave driver like Miss Sparrow wielding the whip, she could come up with a passable essay once in a while. It was perfectly true, too, that for years she had been in the habit of making up stories to tell herself after she went to bed, usually long complicated narratives about a large interesting family who lived in a big old house like the Pettebones', and as she grew older, she had come to think of these stories as novels. But getting them down on paper was not only terribly hard work, and chillingly disillusioning—it was just utterly boring. All the fizz had gone out of them, as out of a bottle of gingerale left uncapped.

Janet looked at her mother, standing there with her head a little to one side, the short curly hair and credulous brown eyes making her look so girlish, though actually she was old—almost forty. Janet felt terribly sorry for her, and loved her almost unbearably, but somehow the two emotions added up to exasperation.

To cover her feelings Janet yawned, stretched elaborately, and said with distant graciousness, "I'll be glad to go for you." She was about to add that some of her best ideas came to her while walking, but something warned her not to.

"Thank you, dear," her mother said, almost fervently, almost as if she had been Louisa May Alcott, for goodness sakes!

Janet took the money and the list, and replied with a shouted "O.K.!" to the admonition, called back from the stairs, to be careful of the eggs and to get the lettuce only if it was fresh.

She slipped out of her shorts and halter and pulled a fresh blue gingham over her head, drew a brush through her pony tail and smoothed her bangs, studying her face rather anxiously in the mirror as she did so, as if it were the face of a stranger. This was one of her Swedish servant girl days, she decided; her cheekbones seemed more than usually prominent, her eyes more than normally tilted up at the corners, and her skin and hair were all one colorless blonde shade. Sometimes she could imagine a famous producer pointing out to an underling in her presence, "Notice the marvelous bone structure," as if she were an exquisite piece of sculpture, but this was not one of those times.

At the front door Janet called, "Mother, get Pudge!"

Pudge was a vaguely bull-doggish creature with a touch of dachshund about the legs and the wistfullest eyes in the world. He stood in front of her now, begging with his stump of tail, and she said sternly, "No, Pudge. No!"

People often stared and sometimes grinned when they saw Pudge, but that was not the reason she didn't want to take him with her today. For purposes of inspiration, she planned to cut through the Pettebone place, and this was a highly clandestine operation which the company of Pudge would make impossible. He always went into perfect hysterics of barking at the sight of the rangy calico cat which patrolled the high stone wall surrounding the Pettebones'.

While her mother restrained Pudge with endearments and murmured sympathy (she used to say he had been an adorable puppy, but that was years ago), Janet made her escape.

Hardening her heart against the dog's whimpers, she thought, *Anyway, I'm a cat person.* Lots of writers were.

Suppose by some miracle (her mother's faith in her, perhaps?) that she, Janet Barnes, should become a famous authoress. Or was everybody a plain author nowadays? Anyhow, she'd get a cat, the first thing. Miss Barnes's famous cat, Xerxes. He'd be featured in interviews. If she were a girl novelist, her mother could hardly go on maintaining, as she had until now, that Pudge was enough pets for any family. Of course, all these supposes were just foolishness. Well, probably they were.

On the way to the market, the part of her mind that was not busy with the future, and with trying, from time to time, to call up a picture of Briar-Rose, was ticking off the houses she passed: Terrill, fake Spanish, the Grays' fake salt-box, new house on the corner, fake ranch.

And then she was across the street, in front of the great ivy-hung stone wall which sheltered the Pettebone place from the city, and her contempt gave way to reverence and love. The Pettebone house was not fake anything; it was unique.

Janet looked at it longingly through the tall wrought-iron gate: a large steep-roofed frame house, magnificently built, beautifully kept up, its size not for ostentation but for comfort and serenity. It was stained a delightful weathered green, the deep porches and eaves were embellished with rich carvings, and in the front a great crystalline window let into the house the green woodland, informal yet controlled, which surrounded the house and covered an entire city block; green of ivy, green of ferns, green of moss, green of grass, and, over all, green of tall flourishing old trees. It was a lovely, lovely place, and Janet adored it—had adored it always.

It was said that Mrs. Pettebone had refused a fabulous offer from the supermarket people, who wanted it for a parking lot, and this alone was enough to make Janet love her, although Mrs. Pettebone was a tall, lean old lady with forbidding eyes whose merest glance was more effective than a dozen no-trespassing signs.

Janet hesitated now, just to one side of the ivied stone pillar which flanked the driveway. The gate was pushed back a little, and she could quietly walk in, as she had rather often done before, dart behind the garages where Mr. Inaba lived (upstairs), take the little path which wound, finally, through a grove of concealing giant bamboo, open the ivy-hidden gate in the back wall, and be in the alley behind the supermarket parking lot in a wink.

But she had to be sure, first, that Mrs. Pettebone and her maid companion were not there. They spent most of the summer at Mrs. Pettebone's Laguna cottage, and part of the winter at a fantastic hotel in Death Valley, so that tiny Mr. Inaba seemed to have the place all to his brown, gnomelike, nearly invisible self most of the time. Never, in all her trespassing, had she and Mr. Inaba encountered each other; she could be sure he was there only because he might be seen very early every morning scrupulously sweeping the sidewalk in front of the Pettebones', and because the lawns and walks and borders about the house were always immaculate.

Janet peered earnestly at the leaf-reflecting crystal windows and the deep porches; she looked to the end of the drive. She wanted very much to take this short cut today, because the Pettebone place, of course, was where Heather and Hawthorne and Briar-Rose spent their secluded lives, shut away from the world by a jealous father.

Only the Pettebone block was not in the middle of town in her story—it was on a great hill, surrounded as far as the eye could see by desolate moors. Hawthorne and Heather were biddable and meek; they spent their days in ladylike needlework, and once in a long while gave tea to the vicar, who was middle-aged and dull.

But Briar-Rose—ah, Briar-Rose was the one who slipped out in the dark of the moon to meet her lover, who had tethered his steed to a lone, wind-stunted tree a mile away, and who climbed over the wall to clasp her in his arms. The lover was—well, she could fill him in later. He had, of course, thrilling dark eyebrows, like Wayne Palmer's, in her math class. She had once begun a poem, on the back of some graph paper, "Thine eyebrows, dark wings fluttering in my heart," and she drew the line out now, as one tries to match skeins of embroidery thread, to see if it might be the sort of thing Briar-Rose would say to her lover. But, somehow, it wasn't. Briar-Rose eluded her still.

Mrs. Pettebone was not at home. Janet sensed it, intuitively, as wild creatures, she thought, know when Man has left the forest.

Nonchalantly, perfectly at ease, Janet strolled in to the driveway, walked half its length, turned into a graveled path bordered by low shrubs, and found herself safely concealed from the house by the garages.

Back of the garages was a tiny kitchen garden, rigorously weeded, exquisitely geometrical, the few vegetables as brilliant and thriving as the illustrations in a seed catalogue. Janet had always found this miniature plot more thrilling and satisfying than the most beautiful flower garden she had ever seen. She would not have dreamed of touching it, but today the smell of ripening tomatoes in the soft afternoon was intoxicating. She knelt to breathe deeply of the scent, so rich, so perishable that tomatoes in the market never retained it, and when she looked up, there stood Mr. Inaba. He was smiling, teeth old ivory in the brown ageless face, but Janet had heard that people of his native islands smile in anger, too, and her heart gave a great startled leap and she scrambled to her feet. What particularly set the burning in her face was the fact that Mr. Inaba would surely take her esthetic appreciation for sheer greedy acquisitiveness.

"Missy Janet," Mr. Inaba asked, in his soft, fluting little voice, "you like kitty cat?"

At first Janet was too startled to answer. She had no idea that Mr. Inaba knew her name, and it made her wonder if there were not other things Mr. Inaba knew, such as her years of secret trespass.

"Oh, yes, I like cats." Janet nodded vigorously. "I love

cats." Her socially awkward position made her more fervent than she might have been otherwise in answer to Mr. Inaba's question.

"Good." The old man smiled even more broadly. "I show you."

He darted into the garages, reappeared in a moment, carrying a wicker basket whose contents he presented for her inspection.

They were three kittens at the darling age, the seductive age, the irresistible age: three gray-eyed kittens, light and dark, soft, perfect, enchanting, as varicolored as pansies.

Janet could not repress a wordless exclamation of admiration and longing.

"You like?" queried Mr. Inaba happily. "You take? Missa Pettebone she come home tomorrow, she no like babies. She say one cat, hunt mice, O.K. Two, three, four cats—no. You want?"

"Oh!" said Janet achingly. "Oh!"

She knew perfectly well what her mother would say, and do, if Janet came home with a basket heaped with kittens.

"Kittens," her mother would say, not looking at them, so as not to have her emotions worked on, "kittens turn into cats, and have more kittens and—no, it is out of the question."

"My mother—" Janet began, "my mother—"

"Good! You take home. You ask mother." Smiling more than ever, Mr. Inaba thrust the basket into Janet's hands.

She looked at him helplessly. She felt completely incapable of discussing her mother's views about cats with someone of Mr. Inaba's limited English and fixed purpose.

Unbelievingly, she found herself walking out the gateway with a basket of kittens over her arm.

At the market, Janet put the basket in a grocery cart just outside the door. She was sure the babies would be all right; in all her life she had never heard of anyone stealing kittens, and when she came back they were still there, two sleeping and the third nuzzling about as if for sustenance.

She moved the kittens over, set the bag with the eggs and the lettuce in one end of the basket, and started home. On the way she cast about for people who might be candidates for kittens, but the results were depressing. Everyone who might possibly tolerate a cat already had at least one.

Janet tiptoed in the back way, put the groceries on the table and the basket behind the kitchen door.

She had only been to the market, and stopped a few minutes at Pettebones', but it was really almost as if she had gone to the Marlowes', or some place as far as that.

Some houses smell so nice, she thought, when you come into them, and ours is one. She closed her eyes for a moment, identifying: scrubbed wood, such a peaceful scent, starched curtains, freshly washed windows, leafy odor of house plants, exciting back-to-school smell of new material from the dining room where her mother was sewing, festive perfume of apples cooked with cinnamon, wholesome yeasty aroma of rising light bread, and yes, even a whiff of Pudge, with overtones of flea soap, from his old rag rug on the back porch. And now, the warm, furry, milky scent of kittens. . . .

"Jannie," her mother called, above the hum of the sewing machine, "just put the things away and then you can get right back to your writing."

"All right," Janet said.

From the basket came a very small mew, tentative, questioning.

Hastily, Janet thrust eggs and lettuce into the refrigerator, took out a quart of milk, warmed some in the smallest saucepan. Testing the milk on the inside of her wrist made her feel grown up and maternal.

When she set the saucer down, on several thicknesses of newspaper beside her desk, she was relieved to find that the kittens already knew how to drink, although they accomplished it with quite a lot of sneezing.

"You darlings!" she whispered. Happily, she looked around her room, and for the first time since she and her mother had done it over, last year, it was exactly the way she wanted it.

Apple-green walls, spool bed bought for a song at a rummage sale, Star of Jordan quilt miraculously fresh and new from an old trunk in the attic, braided rug they'd spent a whole winter making, unbleached muslin prim at the windows—it had been charming, and yet something had been lacking.

"Samplers?" her mother had wondered.

"Kittens," thought Janet. But she would not have dared say it to her mother, so soft-hearted, even foolishly soft-hearted, so understanding about all else, but adamant where kittens were concerned.

All three were still gathered around the saucer, front legs spraddled, tails up, busily lapping with exquisite pink tongues, when Janet's mother opened the door, this time without knocking.

She was very stern, the little line between her brows a deep crease of displeasure.

"Janet, what is the meaning of this?"

Janet began to explain, and it took a painfully long time, because she had to explain about Mr. Inaba too, and the inspiration of Pettebones', and finally even about her trespassing, but amazingly her mother brushed all that aside and returned to the kittens.

"We've been all over the subject of cats before," she said, "and you can't have them."

"But Mother!" Janet began to cry and, even as she gasped out the words, she realized she had been inspired finally to say what she thought she would never have the courage to say.

"Mother," Janet gasped, "would you mind very much if I didn't have any talent for writing? Because I don't, you know."

"Oh, but Jannie!" Her mother's eyes became large and

indignant. "Of course you do. I know you do! And Miss Sparrow thinks so. And lots of people."

"But I don't," Janet said. "At least, most of the time I don't, anyway. Scribbling away up here just to get out of the dishes or something. That's not talent."

Was it amusement rippling her mother's face, a smile trembling at the corners of her mouth?

"Even great writers don't turn out masterpieces every time, Jannie," she said, her expression now carefully grave, "and practice is so important. But you've got years yet to decide what you want to do with your life."

"Oh, I've decided that," Janet said. "The main part, I mean. Of course I want to write, or paint. If I could carry a tune I suppose I'd like to sing. And when I read about Madame Curie, I'd love to be a scientist. But mainly—"

"Yes, dear?" Her mother had an irresistible way, sometimes, of sort of listening with her eyes, as if she couldn't wait to hear the rest, you were so wonderful to be saying what you were saying.

"Well, of course," Janet went on, "anybody can do the wife and mother bit, but (I'm not saying this just to butter you up) I'd sort of like to do it the way you do, with a house that smells happy, and that feels like such a good place to be when you walk in, and my husband—you know how, if we're not there to meet him when he comes home, Daddy always calls out, 'Where're my girls?' and his voice sounds sort of the way I feel when I wake up and it's my birthday. Well, I'd like him to sound like that when he comes home, and I'd like quite a few children, and to remember how I felt when I was a child, the way you do with me."

"The way I do sometimes, Jannie." Her mother sat down beside her on the bed, and her face sort of crumpled out of focus, and her eyes filled with tears, and Janet thought, *Oh dear, why did I say that about the children?* Her mother had wanted lots of babies, too. It wasn't her fault Janet was the only one.

One of the kittens sneezed, a tiny dainty sneeze, and then turned and danced stiff-legged toward them, its fuzzy round head cocked toward the strange voices.

Janet's mother leaned over, scooped up the kitten, held it with absent tenderness against her shoulder, smoothing its head with one finger as she spoke, her voice sounding rather as if she had a cold.

"I'll kick myself. I know I'll kick myself a thousand times. But you'd better get a box, a shallow box, and fill it with sand, and put it in the corner there, and keep them in your room until they're trained. It'll be quite a lot of work, Jannie."

"Oh, Mother!" Her mother's answering hug told her that everything was all right now.

After the box was in place and Janet had cleaned up after the kittens—twice—her eyes fell on the beginning of her story, deserted on her desk:

Old Mr. Marlowe had three daughters—

She read it through, thinking that it started off very well, and that if she came across a story beginning with that sentence she would want to read it. She still believed that was a good criterion of interesting writing, although Miss Sparrow had objected to her theory with a brusque, "Nonsense, Janet! You're a print addict. You'd read anything— the telephone directory if you didn't have something better handy. I know. I'm that way myself."

Maybe, Janet mused, she really did have talent. Maybe, some day . . .

She could see herself, hair coiled into a crown, wearing a pink cotton with a starchy white apron, in a dreamy colonial kitchen, with all the latest gadgets built into brick and natural wood, wielding a long-handled spoon in something delicious steaming on the range, and dashing to a typewriter at an appealing antique desk to tap out a few sentences. At the end of the long sunny room, you could see, through brightly painted bars like the bars on a fairy-tale circus cage, a delightful playroom where an enchanting little dark-haired girl and a sturdy little blond boy played quietly with blocks and a hobby horse.

It was a much lovelier picture, really, than the one of the lady author all alone with her cat.

Smiling to herself, Janet crumpled the paper slowly in her hand and dropped it into the wastebasket without a qualm.

Then she gathered up the kittens, gently, because of the milk-distended tummies, and sitting cross-legged on the bed, she cuddled them on her lap. Oh, infinitely soft and warm and sweet! She seemed to have been missing their warmth and softness all her life. She had not felt so happy, so childishly and lightheartedly happy, for months—not since before the darned old essay contest.

Heather was the light one, Hawthorne was the dark one, and Briar-Rose—Briar-Rose was the color of new rust, tufted with little creamy silver splotches, and with silver feet.

10

Andy Nolan's Gone to Sea

"MAMA, I'm going!"

My mother looked up from the gloss of my father's Sunday shirt to see if I had changed from school clothes to everyday.

"Well, all right," she said. She set the iron on end and rubbed the back of her neck. Her round face was flushed; her pretty brown hair, brushed back with such discipline that morning, curled damply about her cheeks. I knew her head ached, but there was a certain air of triumph about her. The hangers of artistically done-up shirts and dresses were like approaching land to the hard-rowing mariner.

I picked up the paper bag containing my comb, toothbrush, pajamas, and a clean cotton print.

"I can't help worrying," she said, frowning, "staying all night, just you and those three little children—"

"Mama," I said, "it's only across the street!"

"Yes, I know, but if anything should happen while you were watching them—"

"I take perfect care of those kids," I cried indignantly. "Mrs. Nolan says so!"

I hurried toward the door. I wouldn't put it past her, even at the last minute like this, to decide she wasn't doing the right thing, whisk off her apron, hand me the iron, and go stay with them herself.

She gave me one of her keen, judging looks.

"You can be awful scatterbrained," she said. "Sometimes when you're playing with them, you don't seem a bit older than they are."

She followed me out to the front porch. She always moved very quickly and lightly for a heavy woman.

"Now if anything goes wrong, 'phone me. 'Phone me right away, promise?"

"I promise. 'Bye." I tried to keep out of my voice my gladness at going. I heard my mother sigh as she went back to the shirt.

At the Nolan's, the work got done too, I thought, but there was an ease, a gaiety about it. They were so young, all of them. My own mother and father were quite old.

My heart always lifted as I approached the Nolan house —a big redwood California bungalow, nothing special perhaps if they had not lived there. It was across the street and three up the hill from ours. After our yard was in dusk, the sun still lingered on its shingled roof and stone chimney, and the top of their tall bay tree, and words would sing liltingly, joyously through my mind, words I had heard little Susan Nolan chanting one day, standing knee-deep in Shasta daisies in her front yard. "Happy, happy, happy," she was singing softly, while the sun lighted her bright hair.

Perhaps, if I had had brothers and sisters of my own, the Nolans would not have meant so much to me. But there was more to it than that. They were, I used to think, like one of those fortunate families in some charming book for children, untouched by loss or hate, or any of the little squalors and uglinesses that are the lot of the rest of us.

The parents were ready to leave when I got there, big Mr. Nolan in his best navy blue suit, fragile Mrs. Nolan in a gray dress and coat with soft dark fur on the collar. I loved everything about her: her queenly carriage, the way she wore her hair, crisp and black as charcoal, in a Grecian knot, the flower tints of her skin, her deep lovely eyes, the way she cared so much about people, about things—yes, about me.

Mr. Nolan, blond, fresh-faced, as serious as his own students at the Teachers College, was nervously going through the contents of his briefcase. He muttered something about a reference and disappeared into his study.

"It's a beautiful paper, Dorothy," Mrs. Nolan said, in the way she had that I so valued, of speaking to me as if I were contemporary and friend. "But every time he thinks of all those bigwigs who'll be listening to him tonight, he has to check another reference."

She did not heap on me any of those fretful last-minute instructions with which most mothers assuage their guilt at leaving their children. Instead, we discussed the painting she had just had framed and hung over the fireplace. She had worked on it for months; often when I passed, the children would be posed on the lawn while she painted. There they were: one golden-haired, one dark, one sorrel, Susan and Gretel and little Andy, bent over daisy chains in a shimmering mountain meadow splashed with flowers. Their

mother's name signed one corner in large childish letters—
Eileen.

"I think it's the most beautiful picture I ever saw in my life!" I exclaimed.

"Dorothy, I'm so glad you like it." From the warmth in her voice, my opinion might have been as important to her as that of a leading critic.

When Miss Hitchins read "My Last Duchess" to us in Third Year English, I recognized Mrs. Nolan at once:

"She had a heart—how shall I say—too soon made glad . . ."

And when the Duke gave his cruel commands, I sat there —oh, shame!—with tears on my cheeks for everyone to see.

"Dodie! Dodie! I thought I heard your boice!"

I knelt and opened my arms and Andy ran to me. Released from my hug he said, "I been loneying for you."

"Loneying" was an Andy word, and made me hug him again and kiss the top of his red head, with its faint puppy smell that even the cleanest little boys get from being in constant motion so close to the earth.

The little girls came in, Susan blonde, clear-eyed and sturdy like her father, Gretel slight and dark and quick, a sweet-faced Gypsy child.

Mr. Nolan reappeared, resolutely snapping shut his brief-case. There were kisses all around.

"Come on, Talisman," Mr. Nolan said, taking Mrs. Nolan's hand, and the children and I hurried out to the porch to wave our farewells, Andy, in my arms, calling "good-by!" long after their old Ford had disappeared noisily down the hill.

Only Susan looked solemn for a minute; no one cried or was cross. There was always so much to look at, to share, to enjoy, when I was with them. I might have been their big sister, I thought proudly—I might have been a Nolan too, when I was there.

Hand in hand, we went out to look at the tiny new rabbits with back-flattened ears, the tight buds on the chrys-anthemums, the ant lions' miniature craters in a box of soft earth on the screened porch.

The little girls were proudest of Andy's number board, hung at the foot of his bed where the alphabet board used to be. Before Andy was three, he would look politely at the pictures in books, but demand intensely, "What's this letter? What's that letter?" until, in self defense, we taught him his ABC's.

Last week, Susan told me, smiling maternally, Andy had declared, after reciting the alphabet, "That's all there is *to* the ABC's. Make me some numbers." So his mother had turned the alphabet board around and had painted big clear numbers in primary colors and black. And now he had begun to name his imaginary mice, of which there were twenty in his imaginary school, with numbers instead of names.

"Eight-Two," volunteered Andy, "bumped Lewis's head." (Lewis was the original imaginary mouse.)

"Oh, dear," I said, "is Eight-Two bad?"

"No, he's good." Andy was indignant. "That's his work."

"What kind of work does he do?"

"Bump work!"

The little girls and I began to laugh, and after a while Andy laughed too.

There is so much laughter in my memory of the Nolans, especially after Andy came.

He was, at first, a solemn enough baby—"Like a sad lit-tle old man," my mother reported. "A real homely baby. Ten pounds—imagine, with that tiny mother—and not an ounce of fat on him. All wrinkled, and bright red, even his hair, what there is of it. And such big features. But I have a notion he'll grow up to be real striking looking. He'll be a wonderful man. I don't know how you can tell with a new baby, but sometimes you can."

The first time I went to see Andy, he knew me. I can't

explain it, but it's true. His eyes, gray-blue in the little angular, lined face, sought mine, looked steadily—deep-set eyes, beautiful with intelligence and recognition.

I can't imagine how I could have looked to him in those days. My face was always red in summer, my hair the color of Golden Bantam corn, and silver wires restrained my large front teeth. Maybe I looked like a big friendly sun shining over his cradle. His fist clasped my extended finger and he smiled, a wavery first smile, and from then on he was mine and I was his.

He was so young when he first called me "Do'" that no one would believe that it was meant to be my name. Only I knew, and Mrs. Nolan.

I was allowed to hold him from the first, to sit in a low chair by the fireplace, rocking and singing:

> "Andy Nolan's gone to sea
>   Silver buckles on his knee,
> He'll come back and marry me,
>   Pretty Andy Nolan.
>
> "Andy Nolan's fat and fair,
>   Combing down his bright red hair,
> He's my love for evermair,
>   Pretty Andy Nolan."

Mrs. Nolan and I shared Andy's preciousness. Other people smiled, too, when I could not resist telling something amazing Andy had said or done—my mother, perhaps, pleased that her early prophecy concerning the child was being fulfilled, or big Jim Nolan, dropping his briefcase by the door to hug the swarming children, laughing and shaking his head at Andy's latest. But it was Mrs. Nolan and I who smiled at each other with a smile that said, "Typically Andy. Oh, rare Andrew Nolan."

There was the incident with Podgie, the gray tiger Tom. Andy, at two, was trying solicitously to share a banana with the cat.

"Kitties don't eat bananas," I explained, and then, recklessly, because there were people, like Mrs. Puckett next door, who thought it wicked of them, "kitties eat birds. When they get hungry, they go catch a bird."

Weeks later, Andy was playing on the wide front porch. Podgie lay dozing in a patch of sun on the top step. A blue jay alighted on the walk and began swaggering under Podgie's very nose.

"Gaht! Gaht!" (Andyish for cat) in a loud stage whisper to Podgie.

Podgie merely blinked.

"Gaht! Gaht!" Andy repeated, beside himself. Podgie dozed on. Even his tail drowsed. The blue jay took off in leisurely fashion, and Andy, furious, socked Podgie.

"Bahd gaht!" There he was, with a nice nourishing bird set right before him, and he wouldn't lift a paw!

There was the time, when Andy was two and a half, that I was allowed to walk the three children in to town to meet their mother in front of the courthouse. Andy stared up at the tall white building, A.D. 1903, with its chalky statues of Liberty, Justice, and other semi-draped virtues arrayed along the top. Astonished, Andy pointed,

"Thee thothe ladieth."

At home, pressed to tell his father what he had seen on this excursion, Andy said, "We thaw thethe ladieth uptown." He added thoughtfully, "They wath very odd."

That afternoon was unseasonably warm; the bay tree in the back yard, the eucalyptus trees along the streets, gave off pungent odors in the sun. I made lemonade and the children drank it, sitting on the back steps.

"Pinkle-purkle, pinkle-purkle, lemonade in the sun," Andy chanted, as I poured out the ice-tinkling drink.

At bedtime, we had to hunt Bobo, the drowsily smiling monkey, and Busby, painted soldier of impeccable military stance, who shared all Andy's sleeping.

"I know," said Andy, "they're in my Vouring Dun." And so they were, in the tall wicker basket back of his father's big chair in a corner of the living room. There were also in there, I noted, a potato masher, two of Mr. Nolan's textbooks, a smooth brown stone, a piece of bark, some chessmen, and assorted dilapidated toys.

The first time I heard Andy's term for his catch-all, I exclaimed, "Wherever did he get that?"

"I don't know," Mrs. Nolan answered, laughing, "but isn't it apt, somehow? Vouring Dun!"

Like many of Andy's linguistic inventions, it gave me the uncanny feeling that the little boy was remembering a language lost in time.

Andy arranged Busby and his old Lion on the sofa; cuddling Bobo against his shoulder, as he himself had been held when he was a baby, he began to walk in a circle, chanting:

> "When I was skating
> I saw a tiger;
> I skated on.
> I saw a mouse;
> I skated on.
> I saw a star;
> I skated on.
> I saw a storm;
> I skated on."

"Andrew Nolan," his father would say to a performance like this, "founder of the Circulo-Peripatetic School of Verse."

I hated to interrupt; Andy's songs often sounded like poetry to me but Mrs. Nolan was strict about bedtime.

The children slept in a huge room upstairs. It ran almost the length of the house, with the girls' small white beds at one end, Andy's smaller bed at the other, and, next to that, a single bed where their mother slept when one of them was ill. Andy had croup sometimes, and when that happened she wouldn't let him out of her hearing until his breathing was easy again. There were window seats on the east, overlooking the back yard, and chests, and shelves for

117

toys and books, braided rugs on the floor, a low rocker for singing a child to sleep. I remember it as a lovely room, warm and safe and happy.

I was to sleep on the spare bed next to Andy. When I came up, after washing the dishes and putting things to rights and locking the doors, Andy was still awake.

But he did not ask for a story. Instead he would tell me one.

"You'll have to tell it very quietly," I said, "not to wake the girls."

Andy turned toward me, hand under cheek, pleased to have me all to himself. "I'll tell you about my school," he said.

A strong wind had sprung up, after the deceitful warmth of the day. It was thrashing the trees, scourging clouds across the moon to leave us in darkness for a spell, then pouring white moonlight into the room.

"Who teaches in your school?" I asked, knowing that I was expected to help the narrative along with questions and comments from time to time.

"Mr. Tack. And Mrs. Tack. Know what Mrs. Tack does?"

"No." (Feigned interest)

"She's always in the parlor, cooking up good things."

"What do you learn at your school?"

"'Rithmetic!"

"How many kids go there?"

"Fifteen. Fifteen kids and twenty mouses. Lewis and Eight-Two and Five-Three and all my mouses and all my kids. Bobo and Busby and Lion—"

I was very tired and the bed was comfortable, more so than my own bed at home, where I sometimes felt utterly lonely in the dark.

The little voice from the next bed, rather deep for a small boy's, animated, went on rising and falling on the well-loved names.

I forced my eyes open. There he lay, his own eyes wide awake, bright hair shining in a flash of moonlight. The wind tried insistently to shake the solid old house, branches raked at the windows. Downstairs, something banged. Perhaps I should check the screen doors. But I was so sleepy, the bed was so warm.

"Go to sleep, Andy," I said, "go to sleep."

From a long way off I seemed to hear him,

"Me 'n' Bobo 'n' Busby're going to sea."

"That's nice," I murmured. "G'night."

I think it was the dying of the wind that woke me. Everything had become very still. Suddenly I was wide awake. I slid out of bed and, barefooted, crossed the cold floor to the little girls. I pulled up restless Susan's blankets and tucked her in, glanced at Gretel, whose small lovely head with the thick black braids scarcely seemed to move from sleeping till waking, then tip-toed back to Andy.

His blankets trailed on the floor. His bed was empty.

"Andy! Andy!" My panicky whisper made me realize how alone I was.

I switched on the bedside lamp, looked under the bed, in the closet, feeling foolish. The door to the hall was open. Still barefoot, I went to the top of the stairs.

"Andy!" The house was very cold, as if a window had been left wide open.

At the foot of the stairs lay Lion, upside down, just as he had been dropped by the little warm hand that swung him by his tail.

The living room was chilled. I turned on all the lights, saw at once the low table, with Andy's reed chair on top of it, pushed to one side of the door. The night latch had been unchained; strong, clever fingers had turned the difficult bolt on the door.

Words came to me, sweetly spoken, "Me 'n' Bobo 'n' Busby're going to sea." And my drowsy, "That's nice."

Andy was not afraid of anything, not dark nor cold nor

strangers. He had never had to be afraid of anything in all his short life.

Shivering, I went to the door, hesitated.

'Phone if anything goes wrong. Promise. And never get to stay with them again, I added. Prove I am scatterbrained, as she said. If I couldn't find him in a few minutes—then, maybe. Resolutely, I went out the door.

I was wearing only a pair of flannel pajamas, washed thin, too short at wrists and ankles. But there was no time to change, no time to hunt a coat.

"Andy! Andy!" The front gate was open. I did not wait to search the yard. Every house except the Nolans' was dark. Half a block away, a street light glowed forlornly.

I could almost feel Andy's warm hand tugging at mine.

This way, Dodie. Let's go up the hill. Andy was a top-of-the-hill person.

I went up the steep pavement, scuffling through dry aromatic leaves stripped down by the wind. The sky was now completely overcast, the air heavy with rain about to fall. Near the top of the hill, asphalt gave way to a path; the path led through the deep night of an oak wood, the trees twisted and flattened by the sea wind.

"Andy! Andy Nolan!" My voice, breathless, panicky, intensified my fright. Sharp sticks in the leaf mold of the path cut my chill bare feet. The light ahead was the night sky and the tawny grass of the hilltop beyond the wood. I was limping, half crying, when I came out into the open.

Ahead of me, on the very edge of the hill, which gave way to a sharp drop over huge boulders, a straight, white-clad little figure stood out against the night. He carried Busby in one hand; Bobo was clasped protectively against his shoulder. The wind, which always blew up here, whipped back his pajamas.

The rain began with a sudden splattering against leaves and rocks. Exultantly, Andy lifted his face into the weather.

"Andy," I called softly, "Andy!"

He turned. "Dodie!" He was happy to see me, and then startled, and then alarmed at the way I clasped him to me and would not let him go.

"Andy, oh Andy!" I was kneeling, holding him tight, crying. Wondering, he felt the warm tears mingled with rain on my cheeks, felt my sobs.

"Don't cry, Dodie. Please don't cry."

"But Andy, I didn't know where you were."

"Didn't you know I'd come back? Didn't you know I'd come back and marry you?"

When finally he was warm and dry, had obediently drunk his cup of tepid milk, and slept, one arm above his head, one clasping Lion (Bobo hung by an ear on the laundry clothesline), I sat by his bed for a long time, listening for the tell-tale cough or hoarseness, the tightened breathing. I felt that I could sit there all night, keeping him safe.

I knew that there had never, since time began, been a little boy just like Andy. I thought of an incident of a few weeks back, when a young mother had come calling with her infant, on his first outing in the world. Andy inspected the tiny creature, still red, wrinkled, bald, eyes screwed shut. Then, perched on a chair next the visitor, he began making polite conversation.

"I'm three and a half."

"Such a big boy!" The young mother smiled.

And then, in a spirit of comradely feeling, a gracious mood of putting at ease, he said, looking at the new baby,
"Once I was born."

He would be someone like Lincoln, when he grew up.

Andrew Russel Nolan? I would say, in an age-cracked voice, *Yes indeed, many's the time I've held him on my knee.* Would I say, *Once I almost lost him, when he was half past three?* No, never. I drew the blanket tighter around me, and shivered.

I was giving the children breakfast next morning when the parents returned, bringing in a fresh dampness of rain, the bitter spicy smell of chrysanthemums pinned to Mrs. Nolan's coat, and the warmth and radiance of their love.

"How sweet you all look, my darlings," Mrs. Nolan said, including me in the darlings. "And how good that breakfast smells, Dorothy." I had timed the coffee just right. Golden brown it bubbled against the glass top of the percolator.

"We didn't give Dodie any trouble. Did we, Dodie?" This was Susan, the conscientious.

"And, Mama, you know what, when Dodie was pouring out the lemonade, you know what Andy said?"

"Me 'n' Bobo 'n' Busby went to sea!" Andy's slow, deep little voice was almost lost in the rippling girl-talk.

"That's nice, Andy." Eileen's loving smile. "What did you say, Gretel?"

I had only to keep quiet. The girls had not wakened, and if Andy spoke of last night again, they would accept it as one of his charming fantasies.

"Well, I better get home," I said. I tried for an off-hand tone, but a slow, deeply painful blush spread hotly over my face and neck.

The trusting blue of Mrs. Nolan's eyes darkened faintly with alarm.

"Dorothy, do you feel all right? Do you have a fever?"

"No," I muttered, "I'm fine." I hurried out of the room. No longer did I feel like one of the Nolans. I felt like a thief, a cheat. I got my paper bag, which now looked shabby and furtive to me, and came downstairs.

At the front door Mrs. Nolan thanked me warmly, beautifully, as she always did, and paid me, a crisp new bill and some solid pieces of silver. The feel of the money in my hand made me sick at my stomach.

"It's too much," I said faintly.

"Nonsense, Dorothy. If anything, it's not enough."

It was still raining, and she loaned me an umbrella, a jacket of Mr. Nolan's, smelling pleasantly of spilled tobacco, and his galoshes. I couldn't have gotten my toes into Mrs. Nolan's tiny pair.

"Don't forget Friday—the concert!" she called. I waved back, signaling that I would remember, and closed the gate after me. The money jingled in Mr. Nolan's pocket and my nausea returned.

Suppose that Andy should open that door again, and wander out into the dark, after his parents were asleep!

I remembered a laughing Mrs. Nolan, catching a laughing, struggling Andy in rain-wet sleepers in front of their house last winter.

"The first sign of storm and out he goes," she said. "Andrew Jamesson! Andrew the Red!"

Well, I could tell them about the door. I could say I caught him opening it before he went to bed. I had told lies before, and doubtless would again for good and sufficient reasons, but I could not imagine myself lying to Mrs. Nolan. It wasn't a question of right and wrong. I didn't know how.

I put out my hand and drew it along the picket fence I was passing, the numbing cold of the rain and the pickets' sharpness easing my sickness.

He's their little boy. They'll just have to watch him. They'll just have to take care of him. I tried the words over in my mind. I could picture the round flat stone I had seen last night in Andy's Vouring Dun. It seemed to have been transposed to somewhere inside my ribs.

My hand closed anguishedly over the money in my pocket. I thought of a conversation with Andy when he had just turned three.

"My duck has a pocket with a zipper," said Andy.

"What does he keep in his pocket?" said I.

"Dollar bills."

"I'd like to meet your duck. I need some dollar bills."

His eyes grew wide, his voice was shocked. "But Dodie, those are the duck's dollar bills!"

I was passing the Pucketts' tall narrow house with the dingy scrollwork on porch and eaves. I saw old Mrs. Puckett peering at me around a white lace curtain. I hurried, splashing a puddle chillingly against my bare legs. My mother said that Mrs. Puckett was lonesome, poor old thing, but I would not let her intercept me with some errand, some bit of gossip, now.

The more I hurried, running almost in the clumsy galoshes, careless of mud and wet, the more I felt that I was being pursued. So strong was the sense of someone—something—on my heels, that I turned and looked back, up the rainy street. I had it all to myself.

Once I was through our gate, I thought, panting, I would be all right. I wouldn't have to go back to the Nolans' ever, any more.

My mother met me at the front porch. "I was just getting ready to phone," she said, frowning at my splashed skirt.

"Here." I pushed the sodden paper bag against her immaculate starched apron. "I forgot something."

I turned and started back to Nolans', almost running, leaving her calling me, "Dorothy! Dorothy, come back here!"

Mr. Nolan let me in, smiling at the jacket and boots until he saw my face.

"What is it, Dorothy?" His deep voice always had such kindness in it. It was one of the reasons his students loved him.

"It's something I have to tell you," I said. "It's something I have to tell you," I repeated—"both of you."

Mrs. Nolan was in the kitchen, dreaming over a cup of coffee. She looked up, welcoming me when I came in, then her smile too faded.

"Why Dorothy, dear, what's wrong?"

I seemed to be getting a cold—my voice was hoarse when I began to speak,

"Mrs. Nolan," I said, standing in the middle of the room, still in the huge galoshes and jacket, "you remember what Andy said about going to sea?"

"With Bobo and Busby?"

"Yes. Well, he did. He really did. Only he told me first. And I said, 'That's nice.' Because you see, I didn't know." The story spilled out, awkwardly, hoarsely, and when it was done I began to cry. Mr. Nolan handed me one of his big handkerchiefs.

When I looked up from wiping my eyes, Mr. Nolan had an arm around his wife, and was holding a cup to her lips. I had not known a face could go as white as hers was then; her nostrils looked pinched, one hand was pressed against her heart. I might not have been there at all, standing in my muddy tracks on their clean kitchen floor.

"Sit down, Dorothy," Mr. Nolan said, his voice so normal and kind that some of my dread lifted. I sat down on the edge of a chair and he poured coffee for me too, although I was not allowed to have it at home.

There came a tumult of scuffling and laughter from the next room and the two little girls marched in, tugging at Andy. They were all wearing yellow slickers and sou'westers; Susan held out Andy's red boots.

"Here, Daddy, you'll have to put them on. We can't. He goes all limp." Andy looked slightly proud that he was such a problem, and relieved at being turned over to his father.

Mrs. Nolan pulled the little boy to her. "Oh, Andy," she whispered. "Andrew Nolan." She held him for a long time, her face hidden against him. The rain drummed gaily on the roof of the back porch. Andy wriggled free, handed his boots to his father. Mr. Nolan was an expert at booting small feet. Three little fishermen trooped out into the back yard.

And then Eileen Nolan, being Eileen Nolan, remembered me.

"Dodie," she said, using the children's name for me out of her tenderness, "could you come early Friday and give the children their dinner? I never seem to get ready properly when I have to keep dashing back to the kitchen." She was smiling ruefully, a slight color coming into her face.

"I don't think I can," I said, flushing. There was a painful knot in my throat, my nose ached, but I didn't cry. "My mother won't let me stay with them any more after —after what happened."

"Oh, Dorothy!" She was silent for a moment. She knew my mother, too. "Well—" she smiled, "I'll ask her anyway. I'll ask her most 'specially. I don't see how the children could get along without their Dodie."

She came to the door with me. The look in her eyes, the pressure of her hand on mine, stayed with me for a long time.

Out in the rain, the little girls were running along the gravel paths. Andy stood on a big overturned box in the middle of the yard, a gallant little shining figure against the pelting rain.

"See my boat!" he called.

"It's a lovely boat, Andy." I sloshed along in Jim's big galoshes, headed toward the gate.

"Dodie, you're my love for evermair!" Andy shouted.

I turned back, walked through the bitter-smelling sodden leaves, hugged his dripping slicker against me, and kissed the red, rain-cold cheek. I didn't say anything. I couldn't. But Andy still was mine, and I was his. And I knew that if I hadn't gone back, he would have been lost to me forever.

VIRGINIA AKIN

was born in Southern California on December 15, 1917, and grew up in Northern California among the pine trees and mountains. Her father, a physician, died when she was seven. Her mother was a teacher and her brother, George W. Harvey, is a marine biologist at the Scripps Institution of Oceanography in La Jolla.

In 1938 she received her Bachelor of Arts degree from the University of California at Berkeley, with majors in English and Spanish.

Since her marriage she has lived in Riverside, California, where her husband, Glen W. Akin, is a chemist for the United States Department of Agriculture.

Of her family she says, "We have five sons and two daughters, and my entire family has always been very understanding about my writing."

The Dream Years, *her first book, is the harvest of many years of work. One of the stories was written fifteen years ago, one less than a year ago, the others in between.*